Ford Murphy was born and reared in Ireland and moved to the US with his wife in the mid-1990s. Since then, they have lived in the greater Washington, DC area. They have three children. *In Time* is the author's second novel in the *Finn Lane* series and is a sequel to *Taking the Town*. A third and final book in the *Finn Lane* series is currently in progress.

Ford Murphy is a pseudonym of the author's grandmothers' maiden names.

To my family. You are everything.

Ford Murphy

IN TIME

AUSTIN MACAULEY PUBLISHERS™

LONDON • CAMBRIDGE • NEW YORK • SHARJAH

Ordering Information
Quantity sales: Special discounts are available on quantity purchases by corporations, associations, and others. For details, contact the publisher at the address below.

Publisher's Cataloging-in-Publication data
Murphy, Ford
In Time

ISBN 9781638292845 (Paperback)
ISBN 9781638292852 (ePub e-book)

Library of Congress Control Number: 2022913150

www.austinmacauley.com/us

First Published 2022
Austin Macauley Publishers LLC
40 Wall Street, 33rd Floor, Suite 3302
New York, NY 10005
USA

mail-usa@austinmacauley.com
+1 (646) 5125767

Chapter One
July 1988
Edgarville, Kentucky

It was only six forty in the morning, but Finn Lane was already hitting the sixth mile of his daily run. The air was both sweet and sticky and seemed to oil his body with a thin, silky film. The one hundred pound specially designed metal backpack that he was carrying cut deeply into his shoulders. No matter how much padding or cushioning he put around the straps, they still shredded his shoulders to the bone and since Finn ran every day, there was no time for any healing to occur. This morning he could feel the blood begin to flow freely underneath his shirt as the pain intensified sharply from a combination of the straps and his sweat on the open wounds.

The six-mile mark of the run was the point at which he hit the high intensity and most punishing phase of his run. He began to noticeably increase his already fast pace and the effort began to show visibly. His breathing accelerated as he kept pushing himself harder and harder. Soon his lungs felt like they couldn't grab a breath from the warm air and they began to heave more and more. The intense lactic

acid built up in his legs as they pounded fiercely on the asphalt led to a sharply increasing pain that was so visceral it almost made him want to stop and cry out in desperation.

Finn kept going, kept pushing harder and harder seeking for that moment when the physical pain his body was enduring finally overcame and superseded the agony of his broken heart. For it was only at that extreme moment that Finn actually felt like he was still living.

He rounded the corner heading to his self-appointed finish line with every part of his body now screaming at him. The mixture of blood and sweat made his soaking shirt cling tightly to his body as he unbelievably increased his pace even more. Finally, as he neared the finish line, he stuck out his hand and touched another hand that was waiting silently there.

The hand belonged to Hank Holder, a grizzled 67-year-old black man, who for the last three decades had sold newspapers, cigarettes, and candy from a little stall in the park. As soon as Finn's hand touched his, Hank immediately pushed the button on a stopwatch. He watched Finn decelerate until he reached walking speed and he knew from experience it would be several minutes before Finn would be able to return to the vending stand as he fought intensely to catch his breath and tried to deal with the trauma he had just subjected his body to.

Hank glanced at the stopwatch and shook his head with concern.

"That boy is trying to kill himself," he said out loud, "and at this rate, he'll succeed."

He looked at the stopwatch again. Another record time. This was the third in the past five days and Finn had set

seven personal best times in his last ten runs. Hank knew the price Finn paid for each of these records and his concern grew.

Hank and Finn had become good friends these past six months. It started when Finn asked him one morning if he would mind using the stopwatch Finn had in his hand to time his run. Hank had responded enthusiastically. He was not used to white folks interacting with him in this way. They wanted their newspaper or their cigarettes sold to them in a suitably deferential manner and that was all.

Hank felt immediately that the tall, broad-shouldered young man with the funny accent and the saddest eyes he had ever seen was different. He was right. As the weeks passed, Finn revealed more and more of his story and it broke Hank's heart to learn about the tragedies he had suffered. Hank also shared details of his life with Finn and a bond of friendship was forged over shared experiences of love, hatred, loss, and sacrifice.

As Finn started to make his way slowly back to the vending stand, Hank served several customers then reached into the cooler for the gallon jug of cold water he kept there for him. When Finn reached him, Hank soundlessly handed the jug to him and watched as Finn chugged deeply. Finn's face was a mass of sweat and his shirt was stained crimson virtually all over. He helped Finn remove the backpack and clearly saw him wince in agony as the straps were literally peeled off his shoulders.

As he was every morning, Hank was amazed that someone could carry this thing on their back for a minute not to mention running eight miles with it. He sighed to

himself but kept his mouth shut. He knew better now than to voice his opinions about Finn's death wish.

"How did I do?" Finn asked finally when Hank had stored the backpack away where it would stay until tomorrow's run.

"Not bad," he replied. "Not bad."

"Come on, Hank, tell me. It felt fast, especially towards the end."

"Well, it was. But I'm not sure that's a good thing but OK, you knocked twelve seconds off the personal best you set yesterday. I know you don't want to hear it, man, but you are killing yourself."

Hank walked over to the bench where Finn was sitting and eased himself down next to him.

"I understand, Finn, I really do but we both know that this won't end well, don't we?"

He could feel Finn begin to shake next to him as his anguish broke through like it did almost every morning. Hank put one arm gently around Finn's shoulder and caressed his head with the other as they sat there in silence.

"Sir, is this nigger bothering you?" a voice loudly crashed into their silent reveries. Hank instinctively withdrew from Finn and moved away several feet. Finn looked up to see a white police officer standing there glaring at Hank. In his time in Edgarville, Finn had observed enough subtle and overt racism to have a sense of what black people such as Hank dealt with each and every day of their lives. He stood up to face the police officer.

"Thanks officer, but we're fine," he responded in an even and measured tone. "My friend, Hank, was just kindly

helping me deal with a bad moment. He's a good man, Hank. I'd be lost without his friendship."

Finn had adopted a non-confrontational posture with his hands by his sides and his body loose. While his tone was also respectful, there was an expression in his eyes that caused the officer to involuntarily move his hand towards his gun.

"Interesting choice of friends," the cop sneered contemptuously, "very interesting. You're not from around here, are you?"

Finn just stood there, his posture still non-threatening, but locked in eye contact with the officer. Finally, the officer blinked and spoke to Hank, "Get me a pack of Marlboros, boy, and be quick about it."

Hank did as he was told. The officer dropped the money on the counter and walked away.

"Y'all have a nice day now," he said with as much bluster as he could force into his voice.

Hank looked at Finn, shook his head and said, "Forget it. That's just the way it is around here. Won't never change."

"That doesn't make it right," Finn retorted angrily.

"No, it don't but it makes it what it is. Go on home now and grab a shower. I'll see you tomorrow."

Finn nodded, then hugged Hank, and walked off to his apartment. Ten minutes later, he stood in the shower as the water from the jets commingled his blood, sweat and tears into a steady stream that flowed to the drain.

"Help me, Julia," he pleaded, "help me. I don't know if I can take this much longer."

Chapter Two

May 1946

Strongville, Georgia

Hank Holder's battered old Ford pickup truck bounced its way slowly along the dusty backroads. It was almost midnight and he was heading towards Strongville having completed a ten-hour shift at Cartwright's Farm. It was a moonless, pitch-black night and rural Georgia, almost two hours from Atlanta along the shoreline of Lake Lanier and in the foothills of Stone Mountain, was no place for a black man to be driving alone at night.

Hank was well known in the local community; he had served with great distinction in the war where he earned the grudging respect of his totally racist white commanding officer for his courage and calmness under fire. When he had come home from the war, he had taken a job as a stable boy at Cartwright's, who were the wealthiest landowners in the county if not in all of the state of Georgia. It was here his skill with horses became quickly apparent.

Hank seemed to have a special bond with them and could calm down the most nervous and aggressive stallion with his soothing voice and hands. Because of this gift,

Lucien Cartwright, whose family had owned the farm for generations and who at one point had over one hundred slaves working there, had promoted Hank to a supervisory position where he now had two white men reporting to him.

In Strongville, Georgia, in 1946, this didn't sit well with a lot of folks and made Hank's life far more challenging on a daily basis.

Lucien Cartwright was just as racist in his views about black people as his neighbors and friends in Strongville but he was also a businessman and a pragmatist. Hank had a very rare gift with horses and Lucien thought he could profit from it. If it meant giving a little extra to Hank along the way, so be it. If it meant ruffling a few feathers in the white community by doing so. So be it too. He had enough power and money to win any battle in this county and he wanted people to know it.

"Don't you worry none about what folks around here say," he stated to Hank when he informed about his promotion. "They won't like it but there's none of them going to do anything to harm you because they'll have me to deal with if they do."

Hank had been initially skeptical that Mr. Cartwright's confidence in his own power was truly merited but after five months with only minor incidents to report, he began to feel more secure about the situation. Now it was all going to be tested as he spotted the flashing police lights approaching rapidly behind him. Hank pulled over to the side of the road and waited. Two Sheriff's deputies approached the car with their batons in their hands. One tapped on the window and Hank wound it down.

"Where do you think you're going, boy, in such a hellfire hurry? You're putting innocent lives at risk traveling at such crazy speeds."

Hank didn't reply at first. He knew better. If he admitted his guilt, he was in trouble. If he disputed it, he was calling the deputies liars and he was in trouble. He knew what was coming and it was better not to add any fuel to the fire.

"I asked you a question, boy. Where are you going at such speeds?"

"Sorry officer," Hank replied quietly. "I was just coming home from Mr. Cartwright's Farm. I work there in his stables and I was just finished my shift, sir."

The deputies looked at each other when Hank had finished responding as if his words had given them second thoughts. Then one of them said angrily, "You better step out of the car, boy. Right now."

Hank did as he was instructed and braced himself for the beating that was to come. *So, Mr. Cartwright had been wrong after all*, he thought to himself.

"Well now, aren't you the uppity nigger who thinks he can boss decent white men around. Well, you know what, you can't and we're here to show you what happens when you think you can," said one of the deputies with a mocking sneer plastered on his round face.

Hank winced as the first blow struck him in the back. He was determined not to go to the ground and he steeled himself to take as much punishment as he could without breaking. The blows came heavy and often but Hank stayed on his feet and didn't let a sound escape his lips.

"That's enough," a deep voice roared cutting into the night. "Stop it now."

The deputies' hands stopped in mid-flight as the realization who the voice belonged to set in. It was their boss, Sheriff Calum 'Crusher' Conway.

"Move away from him," Crusher Conway ordered. "Get in your car and drive back to the station. Wait for me there. I'll be along presently."

The deputies didn't argue. They left soundlessly without a glance at either Hank or their boss. Crusher Conway was six foot five, two hundred and sixty pounds with a hair-trigger temper that was legendary across the county. He was the last man you ever wanted to cross, not if you valued your life.

"You okay?" Crusher said to Hank. "I heard those two fools often lie in wait for folks like you to come along so I decided to check it out for myself. Lucky for you I did. Old Lucien Cartwright is going to be none too pleased when he finds out what happened to his best stable boy."

"I'm fine, Sheriff," Hank answered. He had been lucky this time. He stretched gingerly assessing what damage had been done. He thought he might have a cracked rib or two but there didn't seem to be anything else broken. "Thank you, sir, for saving me."

"Like I said, old Lucien Cartwright wouldn't be best pleased with the Sheriff's Department if his best nigger got too hurt to work. Besides, boy, you served your country well. That counts for something in my book."

Crusher Conway had also fought in the war and he had lost two of his brothers in France. This kind of thing mattered to him. It gave Hank some extra rights that ordinary niggers didn't get to enjoy in his book.

"Go on home now. I'll drive behind you to make sure there are no more problems," Crusher said as he walked to his car. "Oh, one more thing. I keep hearing these rumors that you are having unlawful carnal knowledge with a white woman. I hope that's not true, boy. We won't abide with that around here. You best keep it in your pants while you still have it and hands to put it there. You get my drift, boy?"

"Yessir, Sheriff," Hank said. "I don't know anything about those rumors but I swear to you they're not true. Honest."

"Well, they better not be, boy. They just better not be."

Hank got into his truck. He was shaking from head to toe and a cold chill engulfed him. The pain from the beating had now fully receded and his mind raced as he fumbled with the gears. He had just lied to Crusher Conway. He was actually in a relationship with a white woman. And he loved her completely and totally even though it would most certainly cost him his life if white people found out. Hell, Crusher had literally told him so directly.

Chapter Three
July 1988
Edgarville, Kentucky

When he was finished showering, Finn sat at the small kitchen table in his apartment and ate breakfast. He had been at Kentech since the beginning of the year and was more or less settled in. Professor Brian Spaulding had responded with enthusiasm to Finn's request for a research and teaching position there. He had been very impressed with Finn when he had spent several months at Kentech as a visiting postgrad student four years earlier and was more than happy to provide him with an opportunity to work there in the chemistry department when Finn had reached out to him late last year.

Finn had taught freshman chemistry this past semester. His classes had proven to be very popular. The freshmen girls were smitten with their handsome Irish professor and many of them invented excuse after excuse to come see him in his office. The freshmen boys were respectful and wary of their young and engaging professor.

They liked his teaching methods and his friendly nature but they had all heard the rumors of Finn's MMA past and

tales of his ferocious workouts in the faculty gym were legendary around campus. So Finn's chemistry classes had been well attended by very attentive and well-behaved freshmen. This was in marked contrast to the experience of many his fellow teachers who struggled with either attendance or discipline or both.

As he ate breakfast, Finn stared, as he did every morning, at the framed photograph of his wife, Julia, and his baby daughter, Siodhraidh. His daughter, who was three months old in the picture, was in her mother's arms and looked like she was smiling perfectly for the camera. Finn had taken the photo himself and knew that it had taken many, many tries to capture that one, single smile. Julia looked so happy in the photo. She was right where she wanted to be, with her husband and daughter. It was the only photo he had of them.

He looked at his daughter in the photo again. He remembered the consternation when he told people what her name was going to be and how it was going to be spelled.

"Don't be ridiculous," his office mate Laura had chided him. "If it's pronounced 'Sheefra', then spell it like that. Why do you want to saddle the poor girl with that useless old Irish spelling? She'll hate you for it when she's a teenager. Trust me, you'll have enough problems with your teenage daughter to deal with. You don't need to add this to the list."

But Finn had been adamant and Siodhraidh it was. Now he sat in his apartment in Kentucky and thought about Laura's words.

"She'll hate you for it when she's a teenager."

He thought about that a lot.

Chapter Four
May 1946
Strongville, Georgia

At the very time when Hank Holder was being battered by Sheriff's deputies, Lillian Cartwright was sitting on the verandah outside her bedroom. The Cartwright family home was an impressive mansion set on a hill overlooking their vast property. Lillian was Lucien and Evangeline's only child. She was now twenty-two years old and was the epitome of a classical Southern belle. Lillian had gone to all the best schools and had been raised to be a lady from the day she was born. She was tall and willowy with chestnut, blonde hair and a perfectly formed oval face with kind eyes and a strong chin. Her voice was as syrupy and sweet as a peach cobbler.

Lillian sipped a glass of her father's good bourbon as she listened to the horses nicker in the stables and the surrounding fields. She loved her horses dearly. Despite her fine features and seemingly gentle demeanor, Lillian was extremely strong and fiercely competitive and liked nothing better than beating the rich young farmer's sons who came courting her over fences or on the flat. Those boys with their

red faces and big ears and stupid stories bored her to tears. She was not interested in any of them.

No. Lillian was in love with a real man. Sitting there, she could still feel the lingering aftereffect in her pussy from Hank Holder's dick. She loved the feel of him inside her, the rock-hard muscles in his back that strained as she held him tightly, and his arms unyielding as boughs as he gathered up. She loved the raw sexual smell that emanated from his body as his sweat mixed with the scent of her sex. She loved everything about Hank Holder; even the fact that he was black and he worked for her father. Maybe, especially that.

Lillian had noticed Hank soon after he had started working at her father's farm. He was different to the other workers. He carried himself with a dignified pride that was so seldom seen in a black man who lived in the South. He was polite and respectful but never cowering or nervous. And, of course, he had that magical touch with horses. It was this gift that initially drew Lillian to Hank and started their conversations.

When Hank was promoted, he now had a lot more freedom to operate around the large barns which gave Lillian more opportunities to be alone with him. It was late one night when they were alone in what was called the Far Barn, because of its distance from the main house, that Lillian kissed him. She had been dreaming about it for two weeks and now finally plucked up the courage.

To her surprise and delight, Hank responded enthusiastically and so the romance began. They had to be so careful that every encounter had to be carefully scheduled and planned well in advance. Despite all of their

precautions, Lillian knew there were rumors among the workers about her and Hank. As long as they weren't caught red-handed, she thought it would be alright. The black workers were never going to tell on Hank and the white workers would not take the risk of telling their employer that his precious only daughter was fucking a black man in his stables. That was never going to happen.

They had been together for almost three months. Lillian had been a virgin and had scarcely kissed a boy before she had sex with Hank for the first time. Now she giggled with delight at the thought of the things they did and how he made her feel. She knew though that it would have to stop very soon. Every day it continued, she was putting Hank further and further at risk.

Trouble was, she didn't want to stop and now there was another complication. Lillian's period was late. She had planned to tell Hank tonight but just seeing him standing there had distracted her so much that all she could think of was climbing on top of him and riding him hard. She rubbed her belly distractedly as she sipped her drink in the cool evening air.

"My, my, Lillian," she said to herself, "what kind of a mess have you created now for us all?"

Chapter Five
August 1987
Lissadown, Ireland

It took Finn over thirty minutes to fit everything into the car. He and Julia were taking their three-month-old daughter, Siodhraidh, for her visit to the beach. It was only a day trip but that still required stocking the car with all of the paraphernalia a three-month baby needed for a successful day out. Finn was still constantly amazed at how much stuff a little baby acquired in such a short period of time. It seemed to him that there were traces of her all over the house, even in rooms that she hadn't actually been in yet.

Still, he wouldn't have it any other way. Her path to this world had been as traumatic as it had been surprising. She had barely survived a shooting in the church on her parents' wedding day and her mother had to fight mightily for them to make it. Finn shivered involuntarily as he recalled how touch and go it had all been and he shuddered to think what would have happened if either or both of them had been lost to him.

Even now, after just three months, he could scarcely remember what his life was like before his precious

daughter had announced her arrival with a loud and piercing scream. His world had changed irreparably the moment he cradled her little body in his arms, terrified that he'd drop her or hug her too tightly. At that moment, he had made her promise that he would always be there for her and he would love and protect her without limits or restrictions.

With the car safely packed, he headed back into the house. Julia had just finished feeding Siodhraidh and was sitting in the kitchen holding her, smiling down at her with an expression of total joy on her face.

"Kodak moment," Finn exclaimed, rushing to get his camera. He knew he drove Julia crazy with all the pictures he took but he didn't care. He wanted to record all of this magic in his life for a later date.

"Now?" Julia retorted in mock frustration. "I look terrible and she needs to be cleaned up and changed."

"You both look beautiful," he said. "Beautiful and natural. So, get ready. Say cheese."

But little Siodhraidh had other ideas. She was not ready to cooperate. So, Finn spent almost ten minutes cooing, whistling, singing, shaking rattles, dancing to get her attention. Finally, for one brief moment, she smiled brightly and Finn snapped the picture just before she turned away.

"Gotcha," he exclaimed proudly. "I do believe this is going to my favorite picture of my two favorite women. I'm going to keep this with me at all times, once I get it developed."

"Finally," Julia laughed. "That took you long enough. I hope it's going to be worth all of the effort you put in."

"It will," he said, smiling at her. "Like I said, I'm going to keep it with me always."

Later events proved this statement true but not in the way Finn intended or could have imagined that morning.

The trip to the beach was a total success. Both Julia and Siodhraidh had fallen fast asleep within ten minutes of them getting on the road. Finn smiled over at them. This is good, he thought. He knew from experience that tired women led to cranky women and that he would invariably suffer.

The weather was perfect and Finn proudly pushed the pram along the promenade, grinning widely at each and every passerby.

"You know other people have babies too?" Julia had said, shaking her head with laughter. "You don't have to strut around like a Cheshire cat. People might think you're a bit daft."

"Let them," Finn laughed. "I'm with the two most beautiful women in the world. It's quite understandable that they'd be jealous."

Later when they arrived home, Julia went to bathe Siodhraidh and get her settled down for the night.

"Open a bottle of wine, will you, love?" she said to him as headed upstairs with the baby. "I feel like a drink and a cuddle. I'll be down in twenty minutes."

When she hadn't come downstairs in forty minutes, Finn crept silently upstairs to find mother and daughter fast asleep in each other's arms on the bed. It was such a beautiful scene that Finn considered for a moment taking a picture. He wisely decided against it, knowing that the flash would surely wake one of them and there'd be hell to pay.

He walked softly downstairs to the living room and poured himself a glass of wine.

He was happier than he thought any person had a right to be.

Chapter Six

May 1946

Strongville, Georgia

Little Maybelle Evans didn't stand a chance. One minute, the little nine-year-old was skipping along the sideway on her way home from school. The next minute she had been scooped up by Billy Ray Schmidt and thrown in to the back of his pickup. There were four of them, Billy Ray, his brother Jimmy, and their cousins—Jason and Harold Thomas. They had been drinking since before noon and now all four were looking to have some fun with some 'nigger ass', as Jimmy put it. They would have like someone older, 'she should at least have tits and hair on her cooch', Jason protested half-heartedly but the boys were horny and Maybelle would have to do.

This wasn't the boys' first time. It was known around Strongville that they had raped and badly beaten at least three other colored girls. Little Maybelle, for all her innocence, knew what was about to happen. She struggled with all her might but Billy Ray just sat on her and kept his hand tightly across her mouth. So, Maybelle lay there, and the stench of sweat and alcohol and her growing terror

caused her heart to beat so rapidly that it felt like it would pop out of her chest.

After about fifteen minutes, they arrived at the Schmidt's deserted barn on the outskirts of town that was down a potholed trail that no one ever traveled. For the boys, this was an ideal location to execute their plans. Jimmy jumped out and opened the doors and Harold drove right in. Jimmy closed the doors behind them.

Billy Ray handed Maybelle out to Jimmy. She squirmed and struggled as best she could but then Jimmy caught her by the hair and soundlessly punched her viciously in the face three times in rapid succession. Stunned, she just dropped to the floor. Jason and Harold watched as Billy Ray and Jimmy ripped her clothes off and carried her over to a workbench.

They were younger than their cousins and a little afraid of them. They enjoyed the protection that came along with being cousins of the notorious Schmidt brothers but sometimes when Billy Ray or Jimmy got mad, they seemed to forget who was family and who wasn't.

"Grab those beers from the truck," Billy Ray ordered as he laid Maybelle face down over the bench so that her butt was just at the edge of it and spread-eagled her. He then roughly tied her arms and legs with rope that he kept there for that very purpose. Maybelle had come to so he stuffed a rag in her mouth to prevent her from screaming. Nobody was going to hear her but Billy Ray knew from experience how bloodcurdling those screams of agony could be and he didn't want that dampening the party.

That had happened one time when the little nigger had screamed with such anguish that Jason had thrown up. No,

across the whole county who bore the scars of his temper. With Jimmy at his side, and having been drinking all day, this could get very ugly very quickly if he didn't do as he was told. Besides, he consoled himself, he was only going to fuck a nigger. Down here that wasn't against the law. The more he thought about it, the more he convinced himself, they were only having fun and it was perfectly legal, the more excited he got.

Billy Ray laughed and said, "Now boys, I think we have us a party going on." He walked over to Maybelle, lifted her head up and looked at her. "Well, little girl, are you having fun yet?" He could see the terror and agony in her face as she fought to catch a breath. The rag was now so far into her mouth that it was almost choking her. Billy Ray let her head drop. "Oh yeah, she's having fun. Jason, your turn. You're going to travel the chocolate highway." Billy Ray laughed out loud. "You gettit? The chocolate highway."

It was over an hour later, just when Harold had finished his second go round that Jimmy noticed Maybelle was dead. She had endured another savage round of beating in addition to all four of them raping her savagely but her heart couldn't take any more and simply stopped beating.

"Damn, Harold, you just fucked a corpse," he sneered. "There's got to be a law against that."

"She was alive when I was doing her," he laughed. "I think she died of a broken heart when I stopped."

"Let's get her out of here," Billy Ray ordered. "We can dump her somewhere on the way into town."

Chapter Seven
July 1988
Edgarville, Kentucky

"I was working that afternoon at old Mr. Cartwright's when my nephew Jackie came to fetch me," Hank told Finn. They were sitting outside on the little deck of Finn's apartment having finished dinner. Finn had been so upset about the incident with the police officer that the next day he had invited Hank over for dinner.

"It's long overdue anyway," he had said to Hank. "You've been such a good friend to me, I should have asked you way before this."

Hank tried to refuse several times but Finn was having none of it.

"You're coming and that's that. There'll be beer and pizza with apple pie and ice cream. Sound good?"

Over dinner, Hank had told Finn what it was like growing in the rural South back then and how the incident with the cop was trivial compared to the true injustice people of color had suffered back then.

"As soon as I saw the wild look of terror in that boy's eyes, I knew something really bad had happened."

"You gots to come, Uncle Hank," he shouted at me. "It's Maybelle."

"I knew that whatever happened hadn't been an accident and I knew she was dead so I just asked the boy 'Where is she' and got ready to go with him. Maybelle was my sister's child. Bright as a button. I remember one time she looked me right in the eye and declared, 'When I grow up, Uncle Hank, I'm going to be President of these here United States of America. Then I'm going to my big, shiny car to come get you so that you can visit me in the White House." Hank laughed. "Imagine that. A nine-year-old black girl in rural Georgia in the 1940s declaring she was going to be President. Heck, maybe might have but the child never made it to her tenth birthday.

"I remember saying to her, 'Hush that kind of talk, Maybelle. Some folks round here won't cotton to it coming from a black girl.' She looked at me indignantly and said, 'I know that, Uncle Hank. That's why I'm only telling you.'"

Hank paused for a minute, took a sip of his beer, looked into the distance as his mind up dredged up what still clearly a painful memory for him.

"Me and Jackie ran as fast as we could and found Maybelle where she had been dumped at the side of the road, not two miles from town. She was just lying there, naked, rag still in her mouth, blood everywhere. Down her legs, on her stomach, and all over her back where the skin had almost completely flayed off her. The agony that poor little angel must have suffered..." Hank's voice choked up as he spoke and Finn could feel tears welling in his own eyes.

"No-one deserved to be treated like that," Hank said angrily. "No-one. Least of all an innocent nine-year-old child. And do you know what the worst part was?" he asked Finn. "The good white folks of Strongville had drove by her lying there for a couple of hours and not one had stopped. There she was naked, rag in mouth, bloody all over and not one Christian had stopped to see if she was still alive.

"It was only when the colored delivery boy for the grocery store had come by on his bicycle that the alarm was raised. He went straight to my sister's house. Only Jackie was home because my sister was at work cleaning the nice homes of white people. After he went to see the body, he had the good sense to come and fetch me."

Hank paused again before continuing, "I just lifted her up in my arms. I didn't cover her or clean her. Poor little thing was as light as a feather. Then we walked like that those two miles into Strongville. My arms were aching by the time we got there, but I wasn't to stop or put her down for a second. Along the way, colored folk came out of their houses and walked behind us. No-one talked or anything. It was a silent procession. White folks just turned their eyes away.

"I remember as we got into town, two Sheriff's deputies stood in our way. I didn't care at that point what they were going to do to me. I was going to keep walking and bring that little angel to her momma's house. Then they just stepped aside to let us through. There was no way they were going to help. They didn't ask what happened or anything. They just stepped aside and let us through.

"As far as those cops were concerned that day in Strongville, no laws had been broken. No-one was ever

charged and those four animals were praying in church the next Sunday in their shiny suits and clean boots. So you see, my friend, yesterday's event wasn't that bad in comparison."

"That's true," Finn replied. "But it was still wrong. Let me ask you a question: did you ever find out who had done that to Maybelle?"

"Oh, I found out alright," Hank nodded. "It wasn't that hard to do."

"And?" asked Finn expectantly.

"And…" Hank looked at him directly, "I took care of it. But I'll need another beer before I tell you how."

"I'll be right back," said Finn and hurried to grab some beers. He was fascinated by the story and he already knew that despite Hank's friendly outward appearance, there was a man in there who would not let the animals who had done such unspeakable things to his niece off the hook. He was certain of that.

Chapter Eight

November 1987
Regensberg, Germany

The receptionist at the Hotel Goliath in Regensberg a picturesque Bavarian town about an hour from Munich, was starting to get frantic. He had been trying to locate the guest in room two-sixteen for the past forty-five minutes to no avail. It wasn't even six-thirty in the morning, still pitch dark outside, but yet this guest was nowhere to be found. They had even used the master key to enter his room in case he was a heavy sleeper and didn't hear their phone calls or the discrete knocking on his room door. It's not like they could bang on the door and wake the other guests up anyway.

He had a very important message to pass on to the guest. The caller, who had essentially roused him from a little nap, almost an hour ago had been completely insistent that he deliver the message urgently. They had checked the little coffee shop and bakery down the street also since many people went there early for breakfast but no luck. The receptionist concluded that the guest must be in a different

room and there was nothing he was going to be able to do until he re-emerged.

In fact, Finn was not in someone else's room. He was out for a fifteen-mile run. He had left the hotel about fifteen minutes before the call had come for him. Even though it was totally dark and quite cold, he was determined to go for a good, long run. He was attending a pharmaceutical conference here in Regensberg and this was the third and final day. It had been interesting and informative but he was now eager to get home to see Julia and six-month-old Siodhraidh. He missed the very sound and smell of his baby girl so much.

He had plotted a course that took him out of the town and into the rolling countryside. Regensberg was in the heart of hops growing country and the fertile ground was filled with little hills and valleys. The hops were all gone now, of course, having been harvested in late summer for consumption at Oktoberfest. Next year's crop would be planted in a couple of months and the cycle would start all over again.

Finn ran easily and fluidly. His body felt strong and his mind was clear. As he made the loop to head back into town, he began to pick up his pace. This was habit. Start strong, notch it up a gear in the middle then go all out for the last portion. He could see the outskirts of the town in the distance.

"I must come here with Julia," he thought. "She'd love it here. There's so much to do and see."

Regensberg was indeed a great place to visit. It was an old historic town with cobble stone streets and an amazing collection of old buildings and bridges. There was a huge

cathedral in the center of the town that was built in the ninth century. It was breathtaking in scale and the level of craftsmanship was truly impressive. He had been told that Regensberg had been spared bombing during the war because it had been extremely foggy the night the Allies had set out to destroy it so they had simply flown somewhere else and never returned.

As he rounded the last corner into the main street, he could hear the various church bells ringing which they all did every fifteen minutes. He smiled. It had seemed annoying at first but he liked it now. He entered the hotel, ready for a shower and that really nice German breakfast that was painstakingly laid out every day.

He headed towards the elevators when he heard a voice call out, "Dr. Lane. Dr. Lane. May I speak with you a moment, please?"

Finn turned to see the receptionist heading his way with a worried expression on his face.

"Oh, Dr. Lane. I am so glad we found you. We have been looking everywhere for you. I have a message. Please call Mike McGill urgently at this number. Do you wish to do it from here or would you prefer to go to your room?"

Finn staggered like he had been hit by a truck.

McGill. How did he even know I'm here? he thought. Then his brain kicked in. He looked at the number. It was his own home number. Why was McGill calling Finn from his own house phone so early in the morning? Then it hit him, hard. *Julia. It has to be Julia.*

He left the receptionist standing there and ran to the stairs which he took three at a time to get his room. He sat on the bed, took a deep breath and began to dial. His heart

was in his stomach by now. Mike McGill answered on the second ring.

"Is that you, Finn?" were his first words.

Chapter Nine
July 1988
Edgarville, Kentucky

Finn sat and looked at Hank expectantly. Hank took his time, his mind clearly wrestling with old ghosts.

"So, see, this is where the story gets complicated," he started.

"In what way?" Finn asked.

"Well, I hope you're not in a hurry because this could take a while. Don't you have to get up early to go running in the morning?"

"Oh no you don't," Finn laughed "No, no, no. You're not using that as an excuse. I have all night."

"All right then. Like I said, the story gets complicated. Right around that time, I was seeing a girl and I got her pregnant. We were young and madly in love. Trouble was, she was white."

Finn let out a low whistle. "I see what you mean about being complicated."

Hank just smiled and said, "That wasn't the half of it. Not only was she white but she was rich white. I mean mega rich. Her daddy, Lucien Cartwright, was one of the richest

men in all of Georgia and he was my employer. Lillian was his only child and his pride and joy. How do you think Lucien was going to react if he found out that one of his black stable boys had knocked up his precious baby? I wouldn't be safe in any part of Dixie back then."

"Tell me about Lillian," Finn asked him.

"Lillian, oh Lillian. She was so beautiful. Everyone loved her. Rich, poor, black, white. She treated everyone nice and was very generous to the poor black kids in the town. Man, she was a looker. And her voice. Her voice was like a honey trap. It just sucked you right in and spread itself all over you with delicious sweetness."

Hank shook himself. "Listen to me, an old fool rambling on like that," but his eyes were still lost in a distant time.

"I remember the day she told me she was pregnant," Hank said then stopped.

It had been just an ordinary day when he saw Lillian heading towards him. There were other people around so Hank knew she wasn't going to speak to him personally. In a loud voice for the benefit of the others in ear shot, Lillian said, "Hank, I'll need the Bay Mare saddled and ready for a long ride at four this afternoon. Please make sure she's ready to go from the Far Barn."

"Yes, Miss Lillian," Hank responded. "I'll have her prepared and ready."

"Thank you, Hank," she replied without making eye contact.

The next few hours seemed to crawl for Hank. He went over to the Far Barn to work on the Bay and he had her all saddled up and watered when Lillian got there.

"Oh Hank," she exclaimed as she buried her head in his chest, "I have such terrible news. I'm pregnant."

Hank held Lillian as her words reached his ears.

"Pregnant"—the implications of that single solitary word were profound for both of them but for Hank, that word could very easily cost him his life.

"Do you love me, Hank?" Lillian pleaded. "Tell me you do."

"You know I do, Lil, but that won't help us now. Not even God Himself could help us now."

"I have a plan, Hank," Lillian said pulling away from his arms. "Just listen to me now. I'm going to leave in the next week or so. I'll say I'm going to visit a friend in Atlanta then I'll just keep on going. I have money and I can sell all my jewelry also. I'll go to Chicago and find us a place. You wait three weeks then follow me. By waiting that long, no one will suspect there's a connection between the two things."

"What are we going to do in Chicago, Lil? Folks up there won't like a black man and a white woman together either," Hank said to her gently.

"No, Hank, that's not true. It's different up North. They may not like it but they allow it. You can get a job and we'll have a nice life," Lillian spoke with such earnest desire that all Hank could do was put his arms around her and draw her to him.

"I think this is a really nice idea, Lil, I really do. But think of all what you'd be giving up just to go live with me in a little shack in Chicago. Look around, Lil, this is all yours. That would be no life for you."

"No Hank, you're wrong. First, I love you and want to be with you. Second, I don't care about all this. I don't. Third, the deed is done now. I can't stay here and produce a colored baby. It wouldn't take long for them to figure out you're the father. Then what? You think my daddy is just going to welcome you into the family? No, Hank. We have to go."

Hank had to admit that she had a point. He couldn't stay here and neither could she.

"OK, Lillian. We'll do it your way. But one thing and I want you to hear about this from me. I intend to kill Billy Ray, Jimmy and their two cousins for what they did to Maybelle. You need to understand that."

Lillian looked at him fiercely. "Hank, I would think less of you if you didn't. Those animals need to pay for what they did. You do what you have to with my blessing."

Hank turned to Finn.

"Such a remarkable woman. There was no fear or hesitation in her life at all."

"What happened then?" Finn asked, totally intrigued by the story.

"Well, a week later she left to visit friends in Atlanta. Nobody thought anything of it. She often did that. But a week later when no one had heard from her, word started to get out that she was missing. Old man Cartwright went crazy. He had people scouring the whole South for her. Her momma just collapsed and had to be sedated. There was all sorts of wild stories going round but none of them involved Lillian Cartwright being pregnant by a black man, and none of them involved me.

"In the meantime, I went ahead with own plans. I made arrangements with a cousin of mine to help me. The plan was I was going to drive south almost to Florida in my pickup, then abandon it. My cousin was going to come get me and take me all the way back up to Charlotte where I was going to catch a train to New York and from there onto Chicago. They were going to be looking for me, I knew this. Not because of Lillian but because of Billy Ray and his gang and what I was going to do to them."

"And what did you do to them?" Finn asked.

He knew all about the need for revenge, the drive inside you that makes you want to confront evil head on and right wrongs. Especially, when it came to the defenseless and the vulnerable. Those are the ones you particularly strive to protect and when they get hurt, you hunt down the perpetrators and take care of things. Finn knew all about this. He lived with it every day and he suspected Hank did the same.

After a long silence, Hank continued with his story.

"I've only ever told two other people about this. One was Lillian and the other is someone who I'm hoping you'll get to meet someday. It was so long ago now that it probably doesn't matter anymore. Anyway, according to the State of Georgia, no crime was ever committed. I'll explain that to you later also. That will take some believing, I can promise you that."

He laughed out loud. "Anyway, I'm digressing. I knew that Billy Ray and his gang always went to the barn where they murdered Maybelle on Friday nights. They'd get themselves plenty liquored up and then go looking for trouble. So, the Friday night before I planned to leave, I

followed them out there. I sat and waited until they had been drinking for a few hours then I simply burst into the barn with my old service revolver in my hand and caught them completely by surprise.

"At first they just laughed at me and insulted me but that stopped pretty quickly when I shot Jimmy right in the face. Billy Ray jumped out of his chair to tackle me and I just shot in both knees. Stopped him in his tracks. I then told Harold to tie everyone up and when he was done, I tied him myself. Once I had double-checked everyone's knots, I went out to my truck and fetched a can of gasoline. You could see the fear in their eyes, even Jimmy's with half his face blown off.

"I slowly doused each of them in gasoline and then I stood there, lit a cigarette and started talking to them, all calm and easy. They were crying like babies, pleading for mercy but I just felt at peace. It was never going to bring Maybelle back but these animals were at least going to suffer something like she did. It felt justified. I stood until my cigarette was finished and started to walk away pouring a trail of gasoline behind me.

"I turned to see them straining and crying then I flicked a lit match onto the gasoline and watched the flame follow the trail over to them. And then they started to burn. It was slow at first and those sounds they made were something awful but I stood and watched until it was over. Then I went outside, set fire to the barn, and drove away. It was that easy."

Finn nodded and thought. "I know what you mean. It is that easy." He had his own stories of justice. One in particular that he thought about every single day.

He turned to Hank. "You did the right thing, my friend. You did the right thing."

Chapter Ten
November 1987
Regensberg, Germany

Finn just sat there on the bed in his hotel room. He was totally numb. His body felt like it just couldn't move. It was almost as if he had somehow been encased in a concrete outer shell that had completely hardened around. He stared at his hands but his brain couldn't make them move. The telephone receiver lay on the floor where it had landed after it fell right out of his hand.

His ears could still hear the sounds of Mike McGill's voice filtering through the phone but his brain could not process any signals to direct any function to his body. So he just sat there, immobilized by grief and shock. Julia and Siodhraidh were dead. Murdered. Their throats cut from ear to ear while they had been in bed. Mike had told him that Siodhraidh was still in her mother's arms when they had found them.

The alarm had been raised by a neighbor at around three in the morning. He was heading to Dublin to catch an early flight to London and was just about to get into his car when he noticed that the front door to Julia and Finn's house was

wide open. He walked over and when he couldn't see or hear anything was just about to close it gently when something made him stop. He knew Finn was out of town and he knew their history.

An uneasy sensation had come over him and he decided to take a look around. He walked in silently and began to look around. Not seeing anything out of place on the ground floor, he moved to the stairs and soundlessly climbed them a growing sense of unease heightening with each step he took. He had opened the door to the master bedroom and immediately saw the carnage on the bed.

Knowing immediately that it was too late to save them, he had rushed downstairs to call the police. Once they had realized whose home it was, they in turn called Mike McGill, who although now retired, was still a powerful presence in law enforcement in Lissadown and his friendship with Finn and Julia Lane was well known.

McGill had arrived on the scene fifteen minutes after he had received the phone call. His heart completely broken by what he saw, McGill rallied himself to deal with practical concerns. The most pressing of which was Finn. McGill had no idea where he could be but he knew he had to locate before he heard of what had happened in the news or, worse still, arrived home to see the state his wife and baby had been left in.

He rationalized that since the front door had been discovered open around three o clock then it was unlikely that Finn had been home and had simply headed into work early or gone on one of his crazy early morning fifteen mile runs. No, Finn must have been away overnight. But where?

Thinking that his absence might be work-related, McGill looked in the phone book for the number of Finn's work colleague, Laura. He reckoned she'd know. If not, given the circumstances, he was sure she'd understand why he phoned her so early in the morning.

It turned out that McGill's instincts were spot on. Laura knew exactly where Finn was and gave him the Hotel name. McGill wouldn't give her any information other than he needed to speak to Finn urgently about a police matter and he that he hoped he could count on her discretion not to spread it around. Laura had agreed but she also surmised that something significant must be wrong.

McGill had the presence of mind to call Aer Lingus and make arrangements for Finn's flight to be changed. He would go to Dublin himself to meet Finn at the airport. First though, he had to make that phone call to Finn.

McGill took several deep breaths, steeled himself, then dialed the number. He was almost relieved initially when he heard that Finn was not in his room. He knew, however, that Finn needed to be located so he urged the hotel clerk to keep calling and checking emphasizing that this was an emergency. McGill sat back and waited.

The crime scene officers had arrived and were going about their business. McGill learned that Julia and the baby's necks had been cut, possibly with a sword, in single, vicious blows. If there was any consolation, it was that they would have died instantaneously without suffering. It wouldn't help Finn to know that now but, perhaps, someday it might. At least a little.

The wait was interminable. McGill was dreading this but he had to take the call. He genuinely loved Julia like a

47

daughter and little Siodhraidh was such a bundle of joy for her and Finn. Now they were dead. Killed senselessly in their own home. It was too much to bear.

Suddenly, the phone rang. The sound was jarring and intrusive. Everyone else in the house stopped what they had been doing as they had been instructed to do so in advance by McGill. Now they just looked over expectantly at McGill who seemed frozen to the spot where he was standing. The phone continued to ring. It seemed almost louder now, more jarring. McGill could sense all of the eyes on him, willing him to pick up.

Then he moved quickly and lifted the receiver.

"Is that you, Finn?"

Chapter Eleven

July 1988
Edgarville, Kentucky

Finn sat in his little office in the Chemistry department building and looked at his watch. It was 8.40 PM already. He shook his head.

"Where had the day gone? You'd think," he thought wryly, "that with the students still gone for the summer, the days would be less hectic."

He was tired and he was hungry. He was also angry. Very angry. The whole campus had just been rocked by reports of an alleged rape and even more shockingly a concerted effort by authorities to cover it up. Although the majority of students were not around, the football team was back and practicing for the upcoming season. This year's team was reported to be very good, the best in years, and hopes were high for a winning season. Something KenTech hadn't enjoyed for well over a decade. The coaches had recruited heavily and it finally looked like a roster had been assembled that would do the college proud.

The story had broken that an eighteen-year-old black girl who worked as a cleaner had been attacked and

viciously raped by three white seniors on the football team. She had been finishing up her shift when she found herself surrounded by the players. They had dragged her into an empty locker room and raped her in turn. They warned her not to say anything, put some money in her pocket, and told her to go home. If she reported it, she was threatened they would simply say that she had asked them to fuck her and no-one would believe her words against theirs.

But the girl, Angeline Evans, was made of strong stuff and she had reported the rape to campus police who alerted the football coaches. Angeline found herself being virtually interrogated in a very aggressive and hostile manner by the chief of police on campus and two football coaches. They essentially reiterated what the players had told her.

It would simply be seen that girl was starstruck and wanted to sleep with the players to get attention. It would be best for herself and her family she was told if she dropped these foolish charges and got on with her life. Her job on campus would be secure and they might even be able to arrange a pay increase for her. If not, then her job would be gone and word would be spread around town about the type of girl she was.

Given how everyone in Edgarville loved their football team, that would not be a good situation for her. The message was clear: play ball and everything would be fine, or else.

After she had left the room, the chief of police turned to the coaches and said sternly, "I think we nipped that one in the bud but you better tell your boys to keep it in their pants from now on. There are plenty of white girls who would

willingly give it up to them with no complications. Tell them to stay away from the niggers, alright?"

Tom Brennan, the head coach, looked disdainfully at the chief, snorted with disgust and spat out, "Do you honestly think my boys would have anything to do with that ratty little nigger girl? She's clearly making it up. I want her gone from this school immediately. I don't care what we told her. She needs to be gone, now."

The chief of campus police, Richard Wiard, was a thirty-year veteran of the force and had witnessed many similar events during his tenure. He took several long pulls from his cigarette before responding.

"You know what, Coach Brennan, I do believe her. I've seen enough to know what's real and what's made up. All I can say is that you better hope this the end of it. If she talks to just one bleeding heart liberal here on campus, football stars or no football stars, this will get ugly. Very ugly. You can trust me on that. Now, goodnight gentlemen."

Wiard got up to leave then stopped and looked around.

"You know, I love this football team too but a girl got raped and none of are willing to do anything about it. If one of our daughters was raped by a nigger, think about what the response would be. Think about it hard when you're saying your prayers tonight."

He stubbed out his cigarette then strode out of the room leaving the two coaches sitting there looking at each other.

If the three men thought that their session with Angeline had put the issue to bed, they were way off the mark. Angeline Evans was just a poor black girl with little education whose job it was to clean toilets and showers for minimum pay but she was a strong, honest girl who worked

hard and who dreamed of bettering herself. She used up a lot of her meager pay to take classes so that one day she too might be able to attend a fine institution such as KenTech. Unlike her friends, Angeline was still a virgin and didn't go to parties, do drugs or even drink. Now all of her plans had been jeopardized by this vicious attack and she was not ready to sweep it under the carpet.

Instead, the morning after her meeting with the police chief and the coaches and two days after her attack, Angeline sat in the office of Professor Denis Desmond, a young liberal Physics professor. She was aware that Professor Desmond had previously stood up for minority students who were being racially abused and she had thought, that while she wasn't a student herself, he might still have the decency to support her.

Angeline was right. Professor Desmond was appalled both by the attack itself and the subsequent attempts to make Angeline feel she was the one at fault or that she was just making it up for the attention. He knew it would be virtually impossible to pursue a legal case at this point against the players but maybe the school could somehow be held accountable.

"I can't promise you anything, Angeline, but I will do my best to make sure that this attack is treated seriously and that those responsible do not go unpunished. I know it won't make what happened right but at least it will send a message that this type of behavior will not be tolerated."

Angeline had thanked him. She was tired of it all now and she was highly skeptical that despite Desmond's sincere intentions all that would happen was that she would lose her

job, the players would go unpunished and she would still have been raped.

Denis Desmond had gone straight to the President's office and demanded a meeting. He recounted Angeline's story in detail and railed about the way she had been treated by the police chief and the coaches.

"It's like she's been raped twice," he almost yelled at the President. "My God, what kind of an institution is this, what kind of people are we that we would put success on a football on a higher pedestal than common decency and human dignity. It makes me feel dirty to know I'm a part of it."

President Browne looked at the worked up young man and furrowed his brow. His immediate thought and his priority was to protect the school but he had to tread lightly. There were other young professors such as Desmond who had joined the college in recent years whose views were a lot more liberal than he cared for and who would certainly see things Desmond way.

"Calm down now, Desmond," he said in his most reassuring but authoritative voice. "There's no proof that anything happened. All we have is that ni…er, girl's say-so. I'll reach out to the Chief Wiard and Coach Brennan and I'll see what they have to say. Give me some time, I'll look into it and get back to you. For the time being, though, best not to say anything about this alleged incident to anyone. We don't want to create scenes where none are necessary."

He had dismissed Desmond and summoned the Chief and the Coaches.

"Pure poppycock," Brennan had exclaimed when the President recounted what Desmond had told him. "The

girl's a liar. I spoke to the players. It never happened. She's trouble and her employment should be terminated immediately."

"Chief Wiard, what do you think?" the President asked. "Is there anything to this story?"

Chief Wiard looked long and hard at Brennan, puffed on his ever-present cigarette then looked directly at the President and said, "Absolutely not, sir. Pure fabrication. I recommend though that we don't fire the girl immediately. We should reassign her to cleaning offices for a few weeks then make a decision once the dust has settled."

President Browne was a little taken aback by this unusual gesture by his hard-nosed police chief. He looked at Coach Brennan who shrugged his shoulders and nodded his head.

"Okay," he declared. "That's settled."

Outside, Wiard turned angrily on Brennan.

"Listen to me now, the next time this happens, nigger or not, you're going down. You understand me? I've bailed your skinny ass out for the last time."

Brennan smiled smugly back at him.

"Hey tough guy, look at how much you make then look at what I make. What do you think is more important around here? In a few weeks, when there are forty thousand fans here paying good money to cheer our boys on, who's job do you think will add more value. Be careful who you threaten. You may not like the fallout."

President Browne never bothered to follow up with Professor Desmond that day or the next or the one after. It was all resolved in his mind so he simply forgot about it. But Denis Desmond hadn't. Frustrated by the lack of

response from the President, he took matters into his own hand and stood up in the staff canteen during lunch and informed his colleagues. Finn had sat there and listened and had become very angry. The response from many of the older and more bigoted staff had been an eye opener for him. Instead of expressing concern for the girl their primary focus was on the reputation of the college and they worried this might be a distraction for the football team's preparations.

Distraction, Finn thought angrily. *That's all they think it is.*

Finn knew firsthand the devastating effects rape had on the victim. He had seen how broken Julia was and how long a process it had been for her to come to trust a man again. Plus, the story that his friend Hank Holder had told him about little Maybelle Evans was still fresh in his mind. This blatant attempt by the college to turn a blind eye was indeed shocking. What Finn hadn't noticed at the time was that someone else had found Professor Desmond's speech very shocking also and determined to do something about it.

Now sitting there in his office, Finn also wanted to do something. He knew he couldn't just walk up to the players and beat the shit out of them, even if that's exactly what he wanted to, but he knew he needed to do something. He couldn't tolerate the idea of innocent people being victimized in this fashion without responding. He never could and he doubted that he ever would.

Without any idea of a plan in his mind, he decided to walk over to the football field where he knew practice would be ending shortly.

Just going to look around, that's all, he told himself. *No big deal.*

When he got close to the field, he could see that practice was over and players were just starting to come of the changing rooms. Standing right of the exit was a very thin young white man holding a bible in his hands and saying to the exiting footballers.

"Repent your sins. The Lord will forgive you. Ask for forgiveness for violating that innocent girl and you will receive God's mercy. He is merciful and will forgive this terrible sin of unlawful carnal knowledge."

Most of the footballers brushed past the young man without looking at him. They were all aware of the situation and the few black players on the team were inwardly furious but unwilling to speak up because they knew they'd be dropped from the team and out of the school if they did. Finn watched as the young man continued to plead with the exiting players.

He noticed that all the players had left except for three, who had hung back. It looked to Finn at first that they were amused by the young man but he could see that after a few moments, their expressions began to change. They started to walk menacingly towards the young man, who stood his ground, bible in hand. There was no-one else around and Finn was in the shadows so he could not be seen by anyone.

"Fuck off, queer," one of them shouted at the young man. "Get the fuck out of here before you get hurt. What we did to that nigger bitch was nothing compared to what we'll do to you."

The young man still stood there, held his bible up, and repeated, "Repent for the sin you have just admitted and God will be merciful."

Finn was impressed with the young man's bravery. He could hardly weigh one hundred and thirty pounds and yet here he was facing three athletes who were each one hundred pounds heavier than him. He was also angry that they so had callously acknowledged what they had done to Angeline and dismissed it like it was of no relevance.

Suddenly, one of them punched the young man hard in the face, knocking him flat. As soon as he was on the ground, all three began kicking him. That was the signal Finn needed. He rushed over, threw himself at the players, and briefly knocked them away from the balled up young man.

"Leave him alone!" he shouted. "Go home now."

The three football players were stunned for a moment but then seeing only one man standing there and their rage fully up now, they charged at Finn all at once. That was their big mistake. They may have been big, strong, and tough but fighting was Finn's game and it took him less than four minutes to put all three of them on the ground with broken bones and shattered egos.

"Holy shit," he heard the young man exclaim behind him. "That was amazing. You saved my life."

Before Finn could answer, two campus police cars roared up, their sirens blaring.

"What the hell happened here?" they shouted drawing their guns as they surveyed the scene.

One of the football players groaned and pointed at Finn.

"He attacked us for no reason. We weren't doing anything wrong. Now we won't be able to play and the season will be fucked."

The officers looked enquiringly at Finn then back at the football players.

"Are you saying that this one man beat all three of you up by himself? Did he use a weapon? He must have, right?"

"That's not true," a voice said. It was the young man with the bible. "They attacked me and would have killed me if he hadn't showed up. He asked them to leave me alone and then they set on him. He beat them fair and square all by himself with no weapons."

The officer's reaction to the young man stunned Finn. He expected them to challenge him but instead they looked at him deferentially and said, "Are you okay, James? We better call your dad."

"You do that, officers," he replied. "I saw everything and they admitted raping that girl. I heard it and I'll testify under oath to that."

One of the officers removed his cap, scratched his head then looked at Finn.

"Did you hear them say that as well?"

Finn nodded. "I did and I'll also testify under oath."

"Shit," the officer spat, "we sure got us a mess now."

Finn turned to the young man.

"Who's your dad?"

"Chief Wiard," came the reply. "I was working in the staff canteen this morning and I heard what was said. I had to do something to support that poor girl."

Finn was even more impressed with the young man's courage now.

"You are one brave man. I'll give you that."

It turned out that no-one had to testify under oath. Chief Wiard broke ranks and supported his son. Enough of the staff had expressed their concern that President Browne, sensing the direction the wind was blowing, fired Coach Brennan and some of his staff. The three football players were expelled from KenTech. A monetary settlement was reached with Angeline Evans. All this happened before the students returned for the Fall Semester and the vast majority were none the wiser.

Finn wasn't entirely convinced that justice had been done but he also knew that this was a big step for a southern institution and that it represented true progress.

Chapter Twelve
April 1947
Chicago, Illinois

It took Hank the best part of four days to get to Chicago from the moment he drove away from the burning barn in Kentucky. He had driven south as planned to meet his cousin, abandoned his pickup by rolling it into a deep lake then doubled back to Charlotte. From there he took a train to New York.

Once he got there, he followed the instructions that Lillian had given him. Hank had been so impressed by her thoroughness and her ability to plan out every single detail so meticulously. Before she left, she had told him that she was going to stay at The Drake Hotel in Chicago under the name of Elizabeth Cantwell and that as soon as he got to New York and knew which train he was coming to Chicago on, he was to leave a message for Ms. Elizabeth Cantwell that HH was arriving on this train number. That was it. He wasn't to ask for her or add anything else. Just that HH was arriving in on this train.

In the meantime, while she was staying at the Drake, Lillian was going to search for a place for them to live. She

had reasoned that a white community was out of the question and that a more upscale black community would be more responsive, or at least not negatively inclined, to a mixed-race couple who were about to bring a baby into the world. Wherever she found, she knew it would be a huge comedown from the style she had grown up accustomed to, and a huge comedown from the elegant Drake itself, but she was ready to make that sacrifice for the man she loved with all her heart and the baby he had created inside her.

When Hank reached New York, he made the phone call as instructed. He had purchased his ticket, had bought himself some food and cleaned up as best he could. He was scheduled to arrive into Chicago that night. He loved Lillian and he desperately wanted to see her but, in truth, he was scared half to death. No matter how difficult his life as a black man had been down south, he knew that the challenges would be just as great, if not greater. Still, he was determined to see it through. It was the honorable thing to do and, besides, it really was what he wanted.

The journey to Chicago seemed to take forever but, at last, with a piercing shriek of its whistle the train finally rolled gently into the station. Hank waited until the other passengers had alighted then jumped onto the platform. There, through the billowing smoke, he spotted Lillian looking anxiously up and down. He walked towards her. He would have loved to scoop her up in his arms and kiss her mightily but, even in Chicago, such displays between the races would not be welcomed.

Instead, he just drank everything about her in with his eyes. She was truly beautiful and there she was standing

there looking at him with such love and devotion, crying and laughing all at the same time.

"Hello Hank," she finally said. "Welcome to Chicago. Welcome home."

"Hello Lillian. You are a welcome sight for these tired eyes. I missed you," he said in response.

"I am so happy you are here. I've found us a really nice place to live and to rear our family. Let's go see it."

They walked out of the station, side by side, close to each other but not touching. There were a few surprised and annoyed glances thrown their way but nobody said anything or made any overt gestures.

If this was Strongville, Hank thought, *I'd be minutes away from being lynched. Here, the worst it looks like that's happening is some dirty looks, and not so many at that.*

Hank also decided that he needed to tell Lillian right away about Billy Ray and the others so he did as they strolled to the bus stop. He told her everything in full detail and didn't omit even the grisliest fact. After he had finished, Lillian turned to him and said, "I'm so glad those dirty bastards got the punishment they deserved. You did the right thing, Hank Holder, and God will understand."

"Why, Lillian Cartwright," he exclaimed in mock surprise, "what would your mother say to hear you use words like that? So unbecoming a fine southern lady."

"Well Hank," Lillian replied in her most demure and genteel voice but with a mischievous grin plastered across her face, "I have no doubt she'd be shocked but I'd say far less so than if I said I can't wait until I get you home and you put your big black dick deep into my very wet and needy pussy."

That shut him up. It was exactly what he had been thinking himself but never in a million years would he have said it out so bluntly as Lillian just had. She stood there next to him at the bus stop, a total picture of complete innocence, and whispered, "Why Hank Holder, I do believe you're blushing and, yes, in case you ask, I can tell even under that black skin of yours. My, my, my. I guess you were harboring the same dirty thoughts yourself after all."

They made love that night as they did most nights until Lillian became too big and too uncomfortable. The months passed quickly. Hank had a found a job at the stables of one of the largest racehorse owners in Illinois. Here again, his skills with those temperamental, highly strung, and very expensive animals quickly marked him out as a really valuable asset and he was rewarded accordingly.

Hank loved his work. He enjoyed the challenge of the horses, trying to understand and interpret the character of each of these sensitive beasts. He was gentle and firm with them and never abused their trust. The hours were long at times, especially when they were preparing for a big race meet but Lillian was very understanding and she knew how important his work was to him and how much dignity this new job had brought him.

They had settled in well to the neighborhood and even though they were the only mixed-race couple around, even if they didn't feel especially welcome, they were never made to feel unwelcome. Hank also knew that several of his male neighbors kept an eye out for Lillian when he was at work and would make sure nothing bad happened to her.

He himself had also spread the word around that the darkest hell would be nothing compared to the fate that

would await anyone who messed with her. He also knew that if the baby were to come unexpectedly, the neighbors would see to it that Lillian was taken to hospital and looked after. All in all, it was as good a situation as could be expected, all things considered.

One day when Lillian was about two weeks from her due date, she walked, or waddled as she herself put it, home from the grocery store. She was so uncomfortable. Her ankles were swollen so much that she struggled to fit into even her most comfortable shoes. She had constant indigestion and felt like she was full of gas. Besides, she needed to pee again for the third time this hour alone. She was so ready to give birth. As was her habit, she spoke to the baby in her womb in a calm and soothing voice.

"Hey there, little baby girl, it's your momma again." Lillian was completely convinced she was carrying a girl and totally dismissed Hank's not unreasonable conjecture that there was an equal likelihood she was going to have a boy. She continued on, "So little girl, I just want you to know that anytime you're ready to come out now is fine with me. I know it's safe and warm where you are right now but your daddy and me are so looking forward to seeing you and holding you. Let me tell you little girl, you are going to love your daddy. He so big and strong and handsome. He won't let anything happen to you ever, I can promise you that. So, what do you think? Are you just about ready to take a chance? I sure hope so…"

Her voice tailed off and she stopped walking. She stood there rooted to the spot. She had been so engrossed in her conversation with the baby in her womb that she was almost home before she looked up to see her parents sitting there

on the front steps. She dropped the groceries in shock and began to sway as if she might topple over. Lucien rushed over to steady her while her mother set about retrieving the spilled groceries.

"Let's get you inside, Lillian," Lucien said tenderly. "You've had a terrible shock. You need to sit down and drink some water."

Almost in a trance, Lillian allowed her parents escort her to the front door. Her mother found the keys in Lillian's purse and they went. Once she was seated and had drunk some water, she looked sternly at her parents and said, "How did you find me? Why are you here? I won't go back with you. You can't make me."

Evangeline Cartwright looked at her husband expectantly and said, "Tell her, Lucien. Tell her."

"Tell me what?" asked Lillian crossly. "I said I'm not going back. This is my home now."

Lucien Cartwright looked at his only daughter sitting here in a dingy kitchen in Chicago just about ready to give birth to a colored baby. Nothing in his life of privilege and wealth had prepared him for a moment like this. Nothing in his life had prepared him for what he was about to say.

"We're not here to bring you back, Lillian. We're here because we love you and because our lives haven't been worth living since the day you ran away. I wish we had been the kind of parents you could have turned to for help and I'm sorry we weren't. I'm not going to lie and say we're not upset and disappointed by the choices you've made and the decisions you've taken. But that's in the past now.

"What's important to us is that we get to participate in your life, irrespective of what way that is. Your mother and

65

I have figured out that we must accept this new reality and be part of it. Otherwise, we lose you and if that happens, we have nothing. Nothing at all."

Lillian was stunned. Never in a million years did she think her father would speak those words but she was also suspicious.

"How do I know you're not just saying that to trick me in to trusting you before you find a way to drag me back to Georgia."

Her mother came to Lillian's side, took one of her hands in hers, and stroked her daughter's hair with the other.

"I understand your skepticism, dear, I really do. But you must believe us. We will never do anything that's against your will nor will we try to separate you from Hank. We know you love him and we accept that. Please give us a chance."

Her eyes brimmed with tears and her voice choked as Evangeline said, "Every day since you've been gone there's been this huge and awful pain in my heart. There were so many days that I wanted to end it all. Now I'm here holding you. I promise you, I won't hurt you. I promise you."

She buried her head in Lillian's lap and sobbed. Now it was Lillian's turn to rub her mother's head.

"I believe you, Momma, I do. And you too, Daddy. Thank you for saying that. I know that can't have been easy."

Just then, the front door opened and Hank Holder walked in.

Chapter Thirteen

November 1987
Lissadown, Ireland

The interval of time, between when Finn heard Mike McGill's voice at the other end of the phone to now, when he stood in the cold morgue in Lissadown looking down at the bodies of his murdered wife and child, had passed in a complete blur. He remembered McGill's voice telling him gently but honestly what had happened. He had sat there for several minutes in silence after hanging up then grabbed a shower, packed up quickly and after checking out of the hotel taken a taxi to the airport.

He had looked out the window of the white Mercedes as the driver had raced along the autobahn at speeds approaching one hundred and fifty miles an hour. McGill had told him that his flight had been changed so he went directly to the ticket desk to collect his boarding pass. Throughout the flight, he had sat immobile in his seat and just stared into space. There had been no tears yet but he knew those would come. There had been no anger or thoughts of revenge yet either but he also knew those would come and they would be acted upon.

He was certain of one thing that when those thoughts of revenge came, they would bring a determination that whoever had perpetrated this crime on his family would suffer consequences of the severest type.

If Finn had yet to shed a tear, Mike McGill had shed many and he did so again when he wrapped Finn in his arms at the arrivals gate in Dublin airport.

"I am so sorry, Finn. I cannot find words to express my feelings."

Finn looked kindly at his great friend, this kind man who had almost been a father to Julia this past year.

"I know, Mike. There are no words necessary."

The journey to Lissadown had been very quiet and now he was finally here with his family. In his heart of hearts, Finn had always feared that something like this might happen. Julia had somehow cheated death twice. He knew the chances of her surviving a third attack were not good. And little Siodhraidh, to think that someone had viciously cut the neck of his bubbly, happy little baby girl was so appalling to him that he couldn't bear to do so just yet.

So he just stood there, next to Mike, and said nothing until eventually he leaned over and kissed both of them. He turned to Mike.

"Julia used to tell me that she wanted to be buried in a quiet little graveyard with a view of the sea and the mountains. I know just the place and that's where we'll put them. Will you help me with the arrangements, please, Mike?"

McGill had nodded. It was all he could do. The lump in his throat was so big that he could barely swallow not to mind speak. He thought of all that Julia had been through

and how happy she had been recently as a wife and a mother. He swallowed heavily and said, "Of course, Finn, anything. Just ask but you know they won't release the bodies until the autopsies have been completed and that will take a few days. I'm sorry."

Finn shook Mike's hand and replied, "I need to go now."

Without another look at his butchered family, he turned and walked out.

Chapter Fourteen
April 1947
Chicago, Illinois

Hank stood and stared at the sight in front of his eyes. The Cartwright's had found them. In the back of his mind, he had always considered this to be a possibility but as the weeks and months had rolled by, he had begun to believe they had actually made it. Now that illusion had been shattered. The Cartwright money had delivered for its masters. His mind vaguely considered how they might have been discovered but his protective instincts quickly kicked into gear.

"Step away from Lillian," he commanded, "and nobody gets hurt."

When no-one moved, he repeated the command. This time with a more menacing tone.

"Mr. and Mrs. Cartwright, I mean you no harm but so help me, I'll do what I have to get you away from Lillian."

To his great surprise, it was Lillian who spoke first.

"Hank, it's all right. I think so anyway. My parents have sworn that they're not here to bring me back to Georgia or to try and separate us. I don't know yet if I fully believe

them but I'm willing to give them the benefit of the doubt. What do you think, Hank?"

Lillian had spoken in her usual clear and logical manner. Hank looked at her then at the Cartwrights and back at Lillian again. He was about to speak when Lucien approached him with his hand out.

"Hank, what I'd very much like now is to shake your hand. As I said to Lillian, her mother and I would rather accept you in your world if we can be part of it than live in our world without her, the baby that's coming and you too. Won't you please shake my hand, son. We're bound together as family now."

Hank could see tears in the eyes of both Lillian and her mother as he stood there. He looked Lucien straight in the eye, squared his shoulders then reached out and shook his hand. It was the first time that either of them had ever shaken the hand of a man of a different skin color. Their grip was firm and sincere, each of them acknowledging the other as a man, accepting that they both truly loved the woman who bound them together.

And while there was no recognition of equality, at that moment it really didn't matter. Equality could come later. For now, a rich white landowner and a dirt-poor black grasped each other's hand in friendship. Hank's almost total disbelief at what was transpiring in front of his was further compounded when Evangeline came and gave him a hug and thanked him for giving them a chance to show they were sincere.

"Okay, Mr. and Mrs. Cartwright, I appreciate that it's very important for Lillian to have you both in her life and if your word is true then I'll accept it also."

Hank wasn't completely convinced of their sincerity and he wasn't ready to trust the Cartwrights' new-found acceptance of their only daughter's situation just yet. He knew the one thing that had hurt Lillian so much was being separated from her parents, after all they had been very good to her and she truly loved them so he decided to play along for her sake. He would monitor their behavior closely though and be ready to make a move if necessary.

"There is one condition though, Hank," Lucien said. "You must call us Lucien and Evangeline from now on. We insist."

Hank nodded. He wasn't ready to take that step yet. He did, however, walk over to Lillian, put his arms around her, and kiss her. If Lucien and Evangeline had an issue with that, there were no outward signs and the smiles on their faces never dimmed.

The next couple of weeks passed by quickly in a domestic bliss that was as welcome as it was surprising. At first, the Cartwrights had tried to persuade them to move to a bigger house in a better neighborhood. Lillian refused point blank and threatened that she would not continue to see them if they persisted with such talk. Nor would they accept any money from the Cartwrights.

So, Lillian's parents turned practical in their thinking and actions. They bought provisions, clothes, and toys for the baby and they helped with the housework. One of the greatest surprises in Hank's life was to see the rich white granddaughter of a large slave owner on her knees scrubbing the toilet where a colored man took a shit every day. Evangeline, who had never so much as lifted a duster

or made a bed in her entire life, found no task to be beyond her in her quest to win her daughter's trust.

The only concession that Hank had made to the Cartwright's money was the choice of hospital where the baby would be born. Hank wanted only the best for Lillian and he knew without a doubt that the private white only hospital the Cartwright's were willing to pay for was a thousand times better than the colored clinic where they would have to go otherwise.

When the day came, Lucien ordered a cab to take them to the hospital and the twenty-dollar bill he slipped the driver quickly silenced any objection he might have to Hank riding in his car. It was the same at the hospital. Lucien hadn't grown up with money and authority without learning a thing or two. He very quickly made it clear that Hank was going to be at his daughter's side and no other option would be tolerated.

Once again, the value of his currency became apparent after he had a private conversation with the hospital administrator. And while of the staff spoke to or even acknowledged Hank, no-one stopped him from going everywhere the Cartwright's went either.

Hank sat with Lucien and Evangeline in the very nicely appointed and private waiting room. It was unclear to him whether they had been allocated this room because of Lucien's money or because of the composition of their party. He didn't care either way. He got up, paced around the room. Sat back down then picked up a newspaper which he threw down after a minute.

"This is the worst part," Lucien said consolingly, "but it will be worth for both of you when you hold that precious

little baby in your arms for the first time. I remember that moment so well with Lillian. It seems like only yesterday but so much has changed since then."

He glanced at Hank hurriedly to see if he had read anything into the words Lucien had just spoken. He hadn't meant any insult and was just about to say so when the doctor came into the room. He looked very flustered. Ignoring Hank completely, he approached Lucien and delivered his awful message.

"I am so sorry, Mr. and Mrs. Cartwright. I sincerely regret to inform you that Lillian has passed. The birth was extremely difficult, the baby was in a breach position and Lillian lost an awful lot of blood. We tried everything to stench the flow after the birth but she kept on hemorrhaging. I'm sorry. In the end, there was nothing we could do. You do have a beautiful and healthy granddaughter though. Seven pounds, eight ounces, and perfectly formed. Would you like to see the baby now?"

Hank let out such a roar of pain that even the doctor asked if he was okay. Evangeline rushed to his side and simply held him. There was so much grief in the room that it seemed to suck the air out of everyone and deflate them so they somehow seemed smaller and frailer. Hank's broad shoulders and broad back now hunched in and his eyes had a haunted look about them.

Just an hour ago, Lucien had been authoritative and powerfully in command of everything around him in the hospital and Evangeline had smiled with the purposeful anticipation of a grandmother-to-be whose daughter and granddaughter would need her support and love. Now they were just an elderly couple lost and uncertain and unsure of

how to hold on as the swirling storm buffeted their weakening bodies and spirits.

Then the spell was broken and the room seemed to steady for a moment.

"I want to see her," Hank said, standing up. "I want to see Lillian."

This seemed to galvanize Lucien and Evangeline who both also stood up. Ignoring Hank once more, the doctor looked at and spoke to Lucien, "I don't think that's a good idea, sir. She's not in a proper state to be seen."

But Lucien was now back in control of his mind and he knew this was another of the many pivotal moments his new life had thrown up for him recently. It was time for him to show where his loyalty lay. His only daughter had just died and he wasn't about to sully her memory or disappoint her now. He set his face to its most determined posture and declared with more force than he thought he'd be able to muster at this point.

"This man is the father of my grandchild. He is my daughter's husband and he has every right to see his wife so you will take him there. Is that clear?"

The doctor looked stunned but nodded. In 1947, the declaration that Lucien had just made were not common words. Even in his state of shock, Hank had heard Lucien say that he was Lillian's husband. He too could scarcely believe his ears. It actually wasn't true. They had known it would have been too complicated so they didn't bother. To hear Lucien Cartwright say those words now made Hank wonder if they shouldn't have gotten married after all.

The doctor led all three of them to the room where Lillian had been moved to. She had been cleaned up and she

wore a fresh nightgown but the pain and suffering she had endured just before her death was clearly etched on her beautiful face. Hank cradled her in his arms and rocked back and forth gently.

"Oh my poor sweet baby girl. What have I done to you? This is all my fault. I'm so sorry."

Lucien put his hand gently on Hank's shoulder.

"It's not your fault, son. It's nobody's fault. You made her happy and she loved you. That's what you have to keep remembering in your heart from this day on."

A nurse brought the baby into the room. She stood there unsure what to do.

"This man is the father," Lucien said pointing at Hank. "Give the baby to him, please."

The nurse paused for just a second before handing the baby to Hank.

"Congratulations," she said a little stiffly. "You have a beautiful baby daughter."

Hank looked down at the tiny bundle lying peacefully in his arms. She was indeed beautiful. Bright blue eyes, with a strong chin just like her mother. It was her skin though that was most amazing. Neither black nor white, it was this in-between color for which there didn't seem to be a word to describe. Hank looked over at her grandparents and reached a decision.

"She's beautiful and I'll love her dearly but I'd like you to take her back with you please. You know I can't rightly raise this girl with that color skin by myself. It would be hard enough if she was black but with that skin color, it would be impossible. That's just reality. No, the way I see

it is she'll be better off and safer with you. Please, I'm asking you."

Evangeline, speaking through her tears, replied, "Of course, Hank, of course we will if that's what you want but won't you come with us? I know it will be difficult but we'll work something out, won't we, Lucien?"

Lucien nodded. "Look Hank, if you're worried about being in trouble in Georgia then let me tell you're not. You haven't committed any crime so there's no reason to worry on that account."

Hank looked at Lucien, his growing respect for the man increasing further. He knew that for Hank not to be wanted in Georgia by the police then Lucien would have had to have pulled some serious strings. He could have just done the opposite and have Hank tracked down, brought back to Georgia and be hung as a killer of white men. Instead, he had used his influence to protect the black man who had made his only child pregnant. At that moment he fully realized how much the Cartwrights loved Lillian and he was even more certain that he had made the right decision.

"I appreciate that, Mr. and Mrs. Cartwright, I really do but, no, I cannot come with you whether I'm a wanted man there or not. Tell her about me and I swear someday I'll come back to visit but you raise her now. One thing though, I'd like her to be named Maybelle. Can you do that for me?"

There was silence for a moment then Lucien spoke, "Alright, Hank, but would it be okay with you if we spelled her name 'Mabel'?"

Hank nodded. He could see where Lucien was coming from. He handed Mabel to Evangeline, went over to the bed where Lillian lay, kissed her forehead, and whispered, "I'll

always love you, my dear, sweet girl, always. Never forget that."

He looked once more at the baby in Evangeline's arms then walked straight out of the room and out of the hospital.

Hank was devastated. He knew his life would never be the same again and that he would never be the same man again. Lillian had defined him as a man. Even just being around her had made him a better person. She was so rare and so beautiful. Unlike almost all other white people, particularly rich southern ones, Lillian's lenses didn't discern color as being of importance. She looked only at character and made her decisions based on that.

Hank knew that there were many white southerners who supported individual black people but had no desire to improve living conditions for the race as a whole. Similarly, he had learned that many good northerners seemed to care deeply about human rights for black people but didn't want to have anything to do with them as individuals.

Lillian was different. He remembered how she lay in his arms after they had made love. The milky whiteness of her skin in marked contrast to the black contours of his body. He thought about the little beads of sweat that always appeared on her forehead, above her lips, and between her beautiful breasts. And how the sweat curled her pubic hair into tight ringlets such that he used to tease her by saying, "You sure yo momma didn't sleep with no black buck now, Miss Lillian? Seems to me we both got the same kind of hair 'cept mine's on my head and yours is on your cooch."

He thought about all these things and the pain engulfed him with a force that was overpowering. Suddenly, the street was too noisy and too crowded, he became

overwhelmed and he knew he was going to be sick. He staggered down an alleyway then threw up again and again. Each violent retch seeming to come from further within his body until he was completely void. He rested his head against a wall and began to sob, great heaving sobs of total desolation. Then he sank to the floor and sat in his own vomit. He had pissed himself.

His grief and his humiliation were now complete. There was nothing to live for now and he had no interest in carrying on. Lillian had been every point on his compass, she had been the moon that forged a yellow path of comfort on the darkest of nights and she had been an invisible cloak wrapping the security and joy of her love around him. Now she was gone. Where was there for him to go now? There was nowhere so he simply decided to stop where he was.

Chapter Fifteen

May 1963
Strongville, Georgia

Lucien Cartwright was fit to be tied. The principal of the very expensive and exclusive boarding school that his granddaughter, Mabel, attended had just called to tell him that he needed to come and collect her, for she was being expelled with immediate effect. This was the third such phone call he'd received in the past year and a half and he truly despaired at what lay ahead.

He had called in practically every chit he had in order to get Mabel into this school and he still had to supplement the already outrageous tuition fees with a very generous donation to school's new library fund to seal the deal such was the extent of Mabel's growing reputation of being uncontrollable. Now it was all for naught.

And he thought bitterly there were only weeks to go the end of the school year. She had gotten so close that he had begun to believe she just might make it. The principal hadn't given him any explanation for her decision to kick Mabel but Lucien didn't really need one. He had probably heard it before anyway.

Lucien sat in his office, swiveled his chair and looked out the open French windows at the vast expanse of his property. He sighed deeply and said out loud, "God help us all. What am I going to do with this child?"

He was getting on now and his health was beginning to fail. Evangeline had passed away four years earlier and he still missed her every day.

"Died of a broken heart."

He had confided just a few days ago to former sheriff Crusher Conway who he played chess and drank bourbon with twice a week.

"Lillian's death rocked her to her very soul but then because Hank gave us Mabel to rear, she rallied herself and that girl became the focal point of her existence. There was nothing that she wouldn't do for that girl. Problem is Mabel is so bad. Evangeline couldn't understand her, couldn't control her, couldn't help her fight the demons that controlled her heart and her mind.

"I tell you, Crusher, it plum wore Evangeline down and she just gave up. Now what am I do? I'm too old and too tired to take her on myself and there isn't a school in the country that will take her if this one kicks her out."

Now it had happened. He was at a complete loss.

He thought back to that conversation with Crusher.

"Where's Hank these days, Lucien? Have you heard from him? Maybe he should step up and take some responsibility? After all, she is his daughter."

Lucien had initially dismissed this. Mabel was sixteen years old and she had never once met her father. She suspected that he was black but neither Lucien nor Evangeline had ever confirmed or denied this. It wasn't that

they didn't want her to know that her father was black, they had just decided a long time ago that skin color was never again going to be an issue in their home.

This was a major evolutionary step forward for these prominent members of the white southern genteel class. True to their new beliefs also they had gone out of their way to improve the lot of their mostly black employees and their families. This did not exactly endear them to their counterparts but Lucien and Evangeline no longer cared what others thought of them.

Besides, they had more than enough money to have the freedom not to care. They knew about the gossip and the rumors that Hank Holder was Mabel's father but they ignored them. Lucien had revealed this information to Crusher who had already suspected as much himself.

Now Lucien thought maybe it did make sense to see if Hank could step in. All this land, this fine old house and all the money would be Mabel's one day. She was going to need supervision and careful watching or else what had been handed down in his family for generations would undoubtedly be blown apart by his wild and unpredictable granddaughter.

He thought about Mabel. Her mother, Lillian, had been a true beauty but Mabel took it to a whole other level. Tall, with a figure that was both sensuous and sexual, she had dark hair that tended to curly but never made it that far and instead fell softly in thick waves down below her shoulders. She had piercing blue eyes that shocked you with their brightness. But it was her skin that made her stand apart.

It was a color unique to Mabel and one that almost defied definition. Light enough in tone that it didn't arouse

any suspicion in white people that she might have a black parent, it seemed to emit a wavelength of understanding to black folk that she was somehow of their kind. Mabel, it turned out, was equally accepted by both races. People gravitated to her, drawn by her looks but enchanted by her spirit. She had grown up in a house free of any racial bias and she herself had none either. She resembled her mother on that score.

Often, it seemed to Lucien that it was almost as if Hank's gift of reaching into horses' souls and calming them had been transferred to Mabel and how she was with people. That was, of course, until it came to those in authority. From her youngest days she had been wild and unruly. Neither Lucien nor Evangeline had tried to impose much discipline but, in truth, Lucien always thought it wouldn't have mattered anyway. She was simply uncontrollable.

Lucien made a decision. He would reach out to Hank and ask to see him. He knew exactly where Hank was and he had kept an eye on him from a distance since Lillian had died. In fact, there were several times when Hank had hit rock bottom that if Lucien's money hadn't been there to help out, it was highly unlikely that Hank would be alive today. It had taken almost ten years of destitute living before Hank was finally able to lift himself out of the gutter and reenter society.

Completely unbeknownst to Hank, Lucien's hand had been there every step of the way to help get there. He was doing well now. Living in Kentucky, he owned his owned newspaper vending stand and made enough money to get by. Sometimes, Lucien would find a new way to chip in some money without Hank ever even noticing. He had made

a promise to his dead daughter that he would take care of the man she had chosen to be the father of her child. It was a promise he had never broken and never would.

Five hours later, Lucien was sitting in the plush office of Stella Leatherwood, principal of the Charleston Academy for Young Ladies. Unable to drive much anymore himself, he had asked Crusher Conway to take him to Charleston to collect Mabel and her belongings. Crusher had been sympathetic but Lucien believed he secretly got a kick out of Mabel's antics or high jinks as he called them and he thought he could see a smile curling at the corner of Crusher's lips as they barreled down the road.

Besides, Crusher doted completely on Mabel who could twist him around her little finger every minute of every day. Fat lot of use the fearsome Crusher Conway had been in instilling any shred of discipline in a sixteen-year-old girl.

"I'm sorry, Mr. Cartwright," Principal Leatherwood had said politely but firmly, "I don't believe this is the right environment for Mabel. Of course, she's extremely popular with the other girls, maybe too popular, and the staff have nothing but the highest regard for her but on balance, I think she'd do much better in a different school with different traditions. I'd rather Mabel herself told you why she's being asked to leave. I think that's a conversation you too need to have yourselves.

"I appreciate all you've done for this school. To be honest, if you hadn't been so generous, I'd have asked her to leave several months ago. I delayed as much as I could out of gratitude and respect for you but now the situation is beyond my control."

She stood up, thrust her hand out to Lucien.

"I wish Mabel all the best and I wish you very god luck."

Lucien took her hand, shook it briefly, and exited the office. He walked to the car where Mabel and Crusher were lounging on the hood smoking and having a grand old chat. They both looked at him guiltily when he stood in front of them. Mabel stubbed out her cigarette, wrapped her arms around him, and hugged him fiercely. He knew for all the trouble she was that she loved him just as much as he loved her.

"I'm sorry, Gramps. I really am."

She looked up at him with her piercing blue eyes entreating him not to be cross with her. And, of course, he couldn't. He shook his head and was about to speak when she giggled and said in a deep voice that was remarkably close to his own, "Now young lady, tell me exactly what I'm supposed to do with you? Well, what have you to say for yourself on this occasion?"

Crusher Conway tried so desperately not to laugh that he ended up snorting out loud which he tried to pretend was a sneeze.

"Bless you, sheriff," Mabel said innocently.

This was too much for Crusher who had had to walk to the other side of the car to disguise his laughter. Lucien himself couldn't help but smile at this terrible child but his smile evaporated instantly when he heard Mabel say, "I'm pregnant, Gramps. That's why they kicked me out."

Chapter Sixteen
December 1987
Lissadown, Ireland

Julia and Siodhraidh were buried on a bitingly cold day in a little rural cemetery in the West of Ireland. Finn had asked for privacy and only invited family and close friends. David Kirk, his oldest friend, was there with his mother and through his grief, Finn thought guiltily that recently he only saw them at funerals. He knew also that being there today brought back painful memories of Margot Kirk who had lost her life trying to save Julia from Morgan Herman's gun on their wedding day. That day, that was such a mixture of joy and tragedy, somehow seemed so long ago in the past now.

As he stood there in the cold watching his wife and baby daughter being lowered into the grave, Finn reflected on how in the back of his mind he had always thought this day would somehow happen. He often felt as if Julia was just on loan to him, there present in his life but somehow not fully anchored down such that they could ride out the storms together.

Based on that thought, he had tried to maximize every single day with her as if he knew that the story of their love

would not be counted in days and nights and years. They had created so many happy memories in their short time together culminating in the magic that was the birth of Siodhraidh. He had sat in the rocking chair in the nursery room on many nights cradling her back to sleep, absorbing the sounds and scents of her little body as they gently moved back and forth. There had been times when his mind had wandered and he pictured teaching her to ride a bike, how to swim and watching her play sports or dance or whatever she chose to do. He thought of how he would console her when some idiot boy broke her heart and how he would one day walk her down the aisle.

Now as she was laid to rest, he knew that's all those would be; thoughts. The incessant pain of it all pounded at him with a force that staggering. Finally, for the first time since they had been killed, Finn began to cry. Big, round and silent tears flowed down his face. He could taste their saltiness as the rolled past his lips and down his neck. He remained standing and the tears kept coming. The ceremony was over. His family was in the ground, in their resting place where they would never grow old. He couldn't move. It was as if he turned and walked away now the connection to them would be broken and he would lose them forever.

Mike McGill and David gently led him down the gravel path to the waiting car. There was a quiet reception planned in a local pub but Finn knew he couldn't go there.

"I want to go home," he said. "By myself, please. You stay. I need to be alone."

So, he went home and sat in the dark in the house where his family had been brutally butchered. It had all been cleaned up but Finn knew he could never sleep in the

bedroom where it had happened. He went into Siodhraidh's room and lay on the floor next to her crib and waited until sleep mercifully came.

When news of what had happened broke around the town, there was a tremendous outpouring of sympathy towards Finn. Everyone knew the extent of the debt they owed this man for saving their town and there was a collective sense of guilt that somehow these brutal murders were their responsibility. There was also a collective determination to try find out who was responsible and make sure justice was served.

The people of Lissadown had rolled over once and allowed their town to be taken over by thugs and criminals. This man had been instrumental in getting it back for them and they were not about to forget that, nor were they ever going to be cowards again.

And so, in the weeks after the funeral, Finn found himself inundated with tips and information about who might be responsible. Most of this information was inaccurate but Finn noticed that one name kept cropping up regularly; Skinny Sullivan, a nasty petty criminal who preyed on the elderly and the disabled and was generally despised as a rat.

Finn never considered for a minute that Skinny was behind the murder of his family, that was way too big league for him, but Skinny had fingers in lots of different pies so perhaps he knew something. Besides, Finn detested creeps like Skinny who only picked on those who couldn't defend themselves or fight back. Whatever he got, he had it coming for a long time.

No smoke without fire, Finn thought. *Skinny is definitely worth have a conversation with.*

One Thursday night in early January, Finn waited in his car outside The Traveler's Inn on Tower Street. He had seen Skinny go in several hours earlier and it was now getting near closing time.

Finally, Skinny emerged. He was feeling no pain. He had sucked back five pints and two short ones and only paid for half of them. He hitched up his pants and decided he would get himself a chicken supper for the walk home and when he got there, he would ride the wife, whether the bitch wanted it or not. He'd belt her a good one if she resisted.

With his plan set, Skinny headed for the chipper at the bottom of the street. Suddenly, he felt this enormous pressure on the back of his neck and then a blinding pain as his face collided violently with the wall. He could feel the cartilage in his nose collapse and his eyes welled up with tears.

"What the fuck," he spluttered as the pain coursed from his forehead to his chin and back up again.

"Who did it?" was all the voice said.

Skinny knew instantly who it was and what the question was about. He had heard rumors that Finn might be looking for him but had dismissed them as idle gossip.

"I don't know anything," he gasped as the pressure from Finn's hand wrapped around his intensified.

Finn's response was to smash Skinny's face back into the wall, this time with more force.

Skinny nearly passed out with pain. He felt his front teeth shatter and blood begin to pool in his mouth. He was nose was fully shattered now and he tried to breathe through

his mouth. All the while, Finn's hand tightened its grip on Skinny's neck like a vice grip.

"Who did it?" was all Skinny heard again.

Struggling now to stay coherent as the pain started to become intolerable, Skinny spluttered in total panic through his tears.

"I swear, I don't know. I had nothing to do with it, honest. You have to believe me."

He had barely finished speaking when once more his face collided full force with the wall. Skinny was in bits now. He had pissed himself twice in the last minute, his head felt like it had exploded and he was in so much pain that if Finn was holding him up by the neck, he'd be on the ground by now.

"Here's the thing, Skinny," he heard Finn say in a cold and calm voice. "This wall will still be here when I'm finished with you but every part of your face will be splattered all over it. You can either tell me now what you know or I'll keep going. I really don't give a fuck either way."

"Okay, okay, I'll tell you. Promise me you'll stop," he pleaded desperately. He had no doubt that Finn meant what he said.

"You have two minutes and Skinny, this better be the truth or so help me I'll make you regret your miserable fucking life was ever created. Start talking now."

So Skinny, with his mashed-up face and stopping to suck air into his bloodied mouth told Finn that the murders had been committed by an advance party of two men from a gang based in Limerick. They wanted to get in and take over the town now that the previous gang had been cleared

out so they had killed Julia and Siodhraidh to make a statement and to show they were not to be messed with.

Finn listened to Skinny's story in silence. He knew Skinny was in so much pain and had so much fear that he was beyond lying to him. Besides, he had heard something similar about a new gang looking to fill the void.

"Listen to me, you little worthless piece of shit. You knew this all along and you didn't say anything. I should finish you off right here and now."

Skinny, now on the precipice of total collapse, pleaded for his life, "I'm sorry. I was scared. I can't stand up to people the way you can."

"Where are they? Tell me now and don't you lie to me."

Skinny told Finn where the gang members were hanging out and promised with his life they'd be there right now.

"Just remember, it is your life," Finn warned him.

He squeezed Skinny's neck even harder as he contemplated whether it was worth hurting him even more for not revealing what he knew earlier and voluntarily. Deciding it wasn't worth it, he let go and Skinny promptly collapsed to the ground where he curled up into a ball. Finn had no concerns that Skinny would try to warn the gang that he was on the way. Skinny was more scared of him right now than anything else in his life.

Finn drove straight to the house where Skinny had said the gang members would be. It was a detached cottage in one of the seedier parts of town, a place where people like them could easily blend in. There was a light on in the living room.

Let's try the direct route, shall we, Finn thought as he exited the car.

He walked rapidly over to the house, paused a moment then kicked in the front door. In an instant, he was in the living room and had delivered crushing blows to the two men there before they had even time to react to the noise of the front door crashing in. Within seconds, after hitting them both some more, Finn had them bound and gagged. The two men looked at him in horror.

They knew who he was but they had believed up until now that there was no way the murders could be traced to them. It was the look in Finn's eyes that scared them the most. It wasn't hate, nor revenge, nor even an expression of murderous intent. No, his eyes had a savage gleam to them that seemed inhuman and chilled them to the very bone.

Finn watched as they struggled with the binds. He knew there was no way they could untie the knots so he began to search the house. Eventually, in an upstairs bedroom, he found what he was looking for. A large, sharp knife encased in a scabbard, it resembled what the Japanese had used in the Second World War to commit hara-kiri. He held the weapon in his hand, staring at the instrument that had butchered the two people who mattered most to him in the whole world.

He went downstairs to the living room. Ten minutes later, he made a phone call and he waited. After a couple of minutes, he could the sirens in the distance start to grow louder and louder until they were right outside the door.

Six policemen converged on the house all at once. As soon as they entered the living room, they were greeted with, "It was us. We killed them. Take us away from him."

The two gang members, having endured ten minutes that would haunt them for the rest of their lives, were more than happy to confess to their crime. Anything to get away from this creature who was almost inhuman.

"This is not the outcome I expected," Sergeant Gerry Brosnan said to Finn as the two men were led away in handcuffs.

"It's not what I expected either," Finn replied, "but enough is enough."

"I'll need a statement from you," Brosnan added. "Tomorrow will be fine."

Finn shook his hand and left. In the following weeks, the townspeople of Lissadown went into action. Signs saying 'NO GANGS ALLOWED' appeared in the windows of shops, offices, and homes. On the roads into town, large signs were erected, each bearing the simple stark warning:

'LISSADOWN IS A GANG FREE TOWN.

NO GANGS WILL BE TOLERATED UNDER ANY CIRCUMSTANCES.

YOU HAVE BEEN WARNED'

The town's message was received loud and clear in Limerick and plans were abandoned. In the meantime, Finn had made plans. His time in Lissadown was up so he set in motion the chain of events that would lead to his relocation to Kentucky.

Chapter Seventeen
November 1963
Strongville, Georgia

"Mabel Cartwright, you get down off that ladder right this instant!"

Lucien had walked into the barn that was being decorated so that it could host Thanksgiving dinner for local poor and underprivileged children. He had been horrified, though not entirely shocked, to see his heavily pregnant sixteen-year-old granddaughter perched precariously on a ladder, stringing lights over the rafters.

Mabel sighed resignedly and slowly worked her way down the ladder that was being held steady by one of the farm workers Lucien had assigned to help and supervise his granddaughter. The worker looked at Lucien and shrugged his shoulders as if to say, "There was nothing I could do to stop her."

Lucien smiled at him. He knew it wasn't his fault. Mabel was determined to hold this dinner and she wanted everything to be perfect. Safely on the ground once more, Mabel walked heavily towards Lucien. She looked radiant, she looked happy, and almost for the first time in her

troubled life, she looked at peace with herself and the world. In fact, Lucien had never seen the child in such a good place. And Mabel's happiness had spread through the Cartwright house, through the farm and into the town enfolding everyone in its path and bringing much needed to where unhappiness had reigned for so long.

Crusher Conway had remarked to Lucien just yesterday, "You know Lucien, this here pregnancy may not have happened in the best way but it has brought so much peace and happiness with it that I'm not so sure it wasn't a gift from God after all."

Lucien fully agreed. Pregnancy had seemed to completely eliminate all the wild demons that had plagued Mabel's life to date. She had become responsible and mature almost overnight and had thrown her heart into improving the lot of others, in particular the poor black folks of Strongville with whom, as she had just recently discovered, she shared a bloodline. She took to promoting and supporting civil rights in her own practical and measured way.

In this, she reminded Lucien so much of her mother, Lillian. Just like Mabel, Lillian was also a doer. Rather than complain about how people were being unfairly treated or discriminated against, Lillian would simply set about finding a way trying to change what was wrong. And now Mabel was doing the same.

It occurred to Lucien that one of the great ironies of life was occurring right now: just when his pregnant sixteen-year-old half-caste granddaughter was fully dedicating herself to dismantling every fabric of life and tradition his family had known for generations, his own life had never

felt on a more secure footing and he himself had never felt so much at ease. Ever since Lillian had ended up pregnant by Hank Holder, Lucien had had to recalibrate so much of his previously steadfastly held beliefs that he was far removed from the man he was twenty years ago.

Looking in the mirror these mornings as he shaved, Lucien felt certain that he was a better man now than back then. He was amazed at the spirit of the females in his family and so very proud of them. His wife, Evangeline, just like him had also cast aside long held beliefs and traditions to accept that her only daughter had given her heart and her body to a black man; his daughter, Lillian, had shown that true love comes from a place deep within and is worth sacrificing everything for and now, his granddaughter had swept all around her up in the force of her quest for good and was bringing them with her on this crusade.

He adopted a stern look and scolded Mabel crossly, "Would you mind explaining to me, young lady, exactly what you thought you were doing climbing a ladder in your condition. I'd really appreciate it if you could help me out here and provide me with a response that makes even the slightest bit of sense."

Mabel simply smiled at her grandfather. His eyes had given him away yet again. Lucien could scowl at her and rebuke her all he wanted, Mabel knew very well this was just her grandfather's way of showing his love and concern for her.

"Sorry, Gramps," she replied with all the innocent sweetness she could muster, "sometimes I forget that I'm carrying a baby."

Lucien harrumphed loudly and gruffly but he completely melted when she put her arm around him and asked, "Well, Gramps, what do you think? Looking good, huh?"

The barn did look good. Mabel had worked hard and as well as the workers Lucien had supplied to aid her, there had been throngs of volunteers who had come out from the town to chip in. That these were all black folks tramping through and around his property didn't seem to bother Lucien one little iota.

When Mabel had first told him she was pregnant that the day he had gone to fetch her from the third exclusive school that she had been unceremoniously expelled from, Lucien had feared greatly for her and for himself. Now, it seemed he needn't have worried. With finding another school out of the question, Mabel would simply have to stay put on the farm until the baby was born. Yet what he had feared most had delivered the most pleasant surprise of his life.

It was almost as if Mabel's pregnancy had pulled open the shutters of sadness and despair that had permeated throughout the household that had started with Lillian's tragic death and continued through her own troubled childhood. Now, it felt like there was a fresh strong breeze in the air that held promise, that held hope.

Lucien was inordinately proud of Mabel and he supported her civil rights odyssey with money and influence where ever he could. This further exposed cracks in his already fraught relationship with his peer group of landowners in the region but he no longer cared. He had his own mission and that was to keep Mabel safe and happy.

The local white townsfolk didn't much like it either when Mabel sat in the colored section of the lunchrooms and diners, used the colored restrooms, and sat with them upstairs in the movie theater. While they grumbled amongst themselves, nobody did anything. She was still a Cartwright and besides, Crusher Conway had made it known that he would take any attack on her personally. Folks around there knew that Crusher was not one to be messed with under any circumstances.

For Crusher Conway, the entry of Mabel into his life had been cathartic in its effect on him. For years, he had been the archetypical racist white southern sheriff. He had kept the local black population suppressed by the threat of and the implementation of violence. There were things in his past that he had done based on his beliefs that nowadays made him ashamed.

He had watched Lucien's and Evangeline's evolution to the tolerant, accepting people they had become initially with a mixture of disgust and respect. But Mabel, who he loved dearly as the daughter he never had, simply carried him along the path with her until he also could look and judge people by so many other facets than their skin color. And just like Lucien, Crusher Conway felt better about himself for this.

One night just a week ago, Lucien had sat on the porch, sipping a bourbon, waiting for Mabel to get home. She had gone to town to work with the local NAACP chapter on the hitherto unthinkable prospect of black voter registration. He looked at his watch, she was running late. He was a little worried, not about her safety per se but about the fact that the child seemed to forget she was six months pregnant and

should be taking it easy instead of rushing all over the county, day and night.

He relaxed once he saw the headlights in the distance beginning to make their way up the long and winding driveway. He took a long sip of the cool and smooth bourbon. Mabel would most likely be fired up about something and would unload the whole thing straight off her chest as soon as she got out of the car. He sighed, steadying himself for the anticipated onslaught. But it never came.

Mabel got out of the car slowly, looking very reflective. She came and sat in the chair next to him. Before he could stop her, she took a little sip of his bourbon and said, "Tell me about my dad, Gramps. I mean the whole story. All of it, okay?"

Lucien looked at her, more than a little taken aback. He wondered where this had come from and why now, out of the blue. Up until now, she had been basically disinterested about the identity of her father. He knew she suspected that her father was black but in never featured as a prominent concern or even thought in her life. Yet here she was, just a few short months before she herself gave birth, asking the question.

Lucien, for a brief moment, entertained the thought of negotiating with her; information about her father for information about the father of her child. He dismissed it though very quickly. It would be unfair to do that to her and he was perfectly fine, anyway, waiting for Mabel to reveal that information in her own good time. He turned to her.

"First, cheeky girl, taking a sip of my good bourbon. It's not for young ladies and certainly not for those in your condition."

"Oh, go on, Gramps. It was just a sip. Now tell me, please."

"Alright but I warn you, it's a long story and it doesn't have a happy ending."

"Well, thank you very much, dearest Grandfather. Here was I thinking that I was the happy ending to that story."

Lucien turned red with embarrassment.

"No, my dear, I didn't mean it like that at all. I just meant about what happened to your mother. Of course, you are the happiest of endings to their story."

"Come on, Gramps." Mabel laughed and gently punched his arm. "I'm just messing with you, that's all. Now, quit stalling and start talking."

So, Lucien did. He took Mabel through the whole timeline of her mother's romance with Hank Holder. How devastated he and her grandmother had been when Lillian had gone missing; how the shock had nearly killed Evangeline. He told Mabel how they eventually tracked the couple down in Chicago and they both laughed when he recounted the shock on both Lillian's and Hank's faces when they first saw the Cartwrights in Chicago.

He described in detail the happy couple of weeks they had spent preparing for Mabel's birth and how they had all chipped with the chores and how good it had felt. The ne described their devastation at the news of Lillian's death. At that point, he reached across to Mabel and touched her face gently.

"You should know," he said, "that losing her made our love for you grow even more."

Mabel looked at the ground and replied, "I always thought that maybe it was my fault that she died and that you and grandma blamed me."

"Oh, my sweet baby girl, look at me," Lucien said. "Don't you ever think that for even a second. It was nobody's fault at all and never, ever for an instant did we blame you. How could we? You are the gift our own baby girl gave us to love in her place."

Mabel shrugged and nodded. After taking a hefty sip from his glass, Lucien told her how Hank had asked them to take her back to Georgia and rear her there. He told her directly how Hank believed that a single black man trying to bring up a girl that looked completely white all by himself was never going to work. Society and the law wouldn't allow it.

Mabel knew more than enough of the world to understand this but she still said bitterly, "Then society is wrong and the law is stupid."

"I know that too now, dear, but I didn't really appreciate then and most people still wouldn't agree with us on that point even today, unfortunately."

He then went on to tell her about Hank. How good a man he was and how much her mother had loved him. He also told her how Hank had suffered badly after Lillian's death and that it had taken many years for him to recover. Lucien also made it clear how proud he was of Hank and how should she be too.

"Impossible love, that's what they had," was how Lucien described it to Mabel. "Impossible love that defied

all of the odds against it and still made it. They were a shining example to us all. They certainly changed my views of the world and I'm grateful for that. Mostly though, I'm so grateful for to them for bringing you into my life."

His voice caught and he struggled with his emotions as he continued, "I don't think I tell you often enough how proud I am of you and how much every day I get to spend with you multiplies the value of my life."

Mabel came and hugged him fiercely.

"I'm sorry I was such a bitch all these years. I don't know why. I think it's because I always felt like I was caught between two worlds and part of neither. I'm going to be good from now on, I swear, Gramps."

Lucien, sobbing with joy and love, just held onto her and stroked her hair gently.

"Would you like me to write him and ask him to come you? I know where he is and I can do that, but only if you want."

Mabel just lay there in her grandfather's arms for several minutes before replying, "I'd like that."

"Great. I'll write him in the morning. Now, young lady, off with you to bed."

"I am kind of tired," Mabel replied. "Thanks for telling me this. I appreciate it."

She kissed him on top of his head and headed for the front door before stopping and turning.

"And, Gramps, thanks also for not trying to use your story to get information about my baby's father. I really appreciate that."

Lucien didn't reply. He just sat there and chuckled quietly after she had gone. That had been a good call. He was glad he had handled it that way.

I'll write Hank in the morning. It's time, he thought. *It's probably too late for him to come for Thanksgiving but maybe he could come for Christmas. That would be nice. Having the whole family together for once.*

Chapter Eighteen
December 1988
Edgarville, Kentucky

It was finally the last week of the semester. The weather had turned noticeably colder in the past two weeks and it was becoming a bit of a struggle for Finn to force himself out of his warm bed in the pitch darkness of the early morning to go on his punishing run. His shoulders had, thankfully, developed enough calluses by now that they no longer bled from the heavily weighted backpack that he wore each day while running but that didn't mean they didn't hurt. They did, every day, like a son of a bitch.

Finn was heading to Ireland for ten days to celebrate Christmas with his family. He had thought for the longest about not going and just staying put here. He really didn't want to watch everyone celebrating and being happy and he knew the sight of little kids and Santa would upset him.

Still, he rationalized, this was something he had to get used to and he couldn't avoid it forever. So, he decided to go. It would also give him an opportunity to visit Julia's and Siodhraidh's grave. As nice as the graveyard may be in the

summer sunshine, it would be dark and desolate during the gray and bleak Irish winter.

He and Hank Holder had become good friends these past few months and Finn had invited the older man over to his apartment for pizza and beers at least once a week. If Finn ever thought it curious that he was never invited over to Hank's house, he never dwelled on it or mentioned it.

When he had asked Hank what his plans were for the holidays, Hank had been vague in his response.

"Oh, not much. This and that."

Finn noticed that Hank was perfectly happy to talk to him about his past, about family members who were all dead now but he never mentioned the living. Finn had the distinct impression that Hank was concealing something though he ultimately came to believe that Hank lived alone and was perfectly happy with that arrangement.

He thought about Hank again this morning as he dressed for his run. Hank had told him all about Lillian's death and Mabel's birth. He had been very graphic and detailed in his descriptions of how his life had progressed from the day he had been slumped in an alleyway in Chicago covered in his own piss and vomit.

Hank had stayed in that alleyway overnight until he was chased out of it by the owner of a business whose back entrance opened out there. He had just drifted for days around the city, not eating much, barely even conscious of what was going on around him. As the days passed, he became dirtier and more decrepit. He was beaten up twice and never once did he try to defend himself.

He welcomed the pain the blows brought to his body as they masked the pain that surrounded his heart constantly.

He was arrested once for vagrancy but released after one night, mainly because nobody wanted anything to do with such a dirty and decaying black man.

Finally, he was spotted by a neighbor who just happened to be visiting the part of town that Hank strayed to. The neighbor hardly recognized Hank at first under the dirt and the filth and the smell coming from him was obnoxiously overwhelming. But the neighbor knew what had happened and he had genuinely liked Lillian as well as Hank, so held his nose and paid his cousin money to transport the two of them in the back of his pickup truck back to Hank's house.

At first, Hank didn't want to go in but the neighbor eventually persuaded him. It then took a while but finally Hank was all cleaned up and dressed in fresh clothes. The neighbor had set about preparing some food when he heard the front door close.

By the time he got there, he could see Hank disappearing down the street, suitcase in hand. He turned once to wave at him and yelled, "Sell or keep whatever you want. I've no need for it any longer."

With that he was gone. He never visited the neighborhood again. Hank had told Finn that on that day, "With clean clothes on and some money in my pocket, that was the best state I was in for the next ten years."

Hank had called them his lost decade. He bounced from odd job to job unable to retain steady employment for very long. He drank too much and he got hooked on drugs several times. He became a complete mess. As he drifted from state to state and found himself in difficult and dangerous situations, it always seemed to him that there was

a guiding spirit watching out for him, making sure he didn't fall too far or get too lost. In his heart, this was Lillian taking care of him but, in his mind, he suspected that Lucien might have something to do with it.

"Eventually," he told Finn, "the fog lifted and I started to see clearly again. I had found my way, somehow, down here to Edgarville, Kentucky. So I decided to stay. After a while, I scraped up enough money to buy the newspaper stand and over time, I added cigarettes, candy, soda, and fruit. Not many white folks were thrilled with me owning that stand but, apart from some minor incidents, I've been allowed to operate there in relative peace."

It was time for Finn to go on his run. He would see Hank in less than ninety minutes after he had completed fifteen miles while wearing a one hundred pound backpack.

Chapter Nineteen
1964
Strongville, Georgia

The Thanksgiving dinner had been a tremendous success. Over thirty poor families had enjoyed a meal, with all the trimmings, that they barely knew existed before that day. Mabel had been in her element, bustling here, there and everywhere determined not to let her protruding belly slow her down. Both Lucien and Crusher had asked her on several occasions to stop and take a rest but Mabel wasn't having any of it so she simply ignored them. She was usually pleased with and touched by their mother hen clucking and fussing around her but that day she needed her space.

It had come as no great surprise to Lucien when Mabel had suggested that they do the same for Christmas. He had agreed readily but his key concern was that Mabel would by then be a month further in to her pregnancy and her due would be looming closer.

He needn't have worried. The day passed without a hitch and Lucien finally realized that Mabel had just instituted two new Cartwright family traditions:

Thanksgiving and Christmas dinner would from now on be hosted at their farm for the poor and the needy. Lucien was pleased at the thought.

"That's a mighty tradition the girl has started," he crowed one night to Crusher Conway. "And she's still only a young girl."

"And pregnant to boot," Crusher had added. "Though I'm not sure that has anything to do with anything."

The only sad part on Christmas was that Hank had chosen not to attend. He had written back to Lucien, thanking him for his letter and the very kind invitation to come and meet Mabel.

"I am truly grateful, Mr. Cartwright, and touched by this very generous offer. It is of great comfort to me that you still place a value upon, and hold in recognition, the family bonds that connect us. I am pleased to hear that Mabel is doing so well. While I share your concern that she will become a mother at much too young an age, I am comforted by the fact that she seems to have inherited so much of her own mother's strength and will power. I have little doubt then that she will succeed admirably at the task of rearing a child.

"I shall be most happy to come visit when the time is right. However, that time is not now so I must respectfully decline this very invitation. I believe we will all recognize when the time is right for that visit and we must abide until that moment.

"Please tell Mabel how proud I am of her as I know her mother is as well."

Lucien had been moved by the eloquence of Hank's response. He wasn't sure he necessarily agreed with Hank

that the time had not yet come for him to meet his daughter but then he didn't walk in Hank's shoes and he wasn't going to criticize him for that decision. He had shown Hank's letter to Mabel.

Her disappointment was written all over face after she read her father's words but she looked up at Lucien and merely said, "It's fine, Gramps, I understand. He'll come when he's ready. I'll be waiting and so will his grandchild."

As Mabel's due date wound ever closer, Lucien sprang into action. She had declared that she wasn't going to a hospital and that she was going to give birth in her own home, in her own room. With the memory of Lillian's death in childbirth still haunting him, Lucien put his money to work. He engaged top doctors and medical staff to deliver the baby and he organized for the latest equipment and medicine to be on hand. He was determined to take no chances on this occasion.

The day finally arrived and Lucien watched his precious granddaughter be led into her bedroom by a highly attentive staff. He and Crusher tried to play chess while they waited but neither of them could concentrate. They kept wandering the halls of the Cartwright mansion, drawn inexorably to Mabel's room from where they would be shooed away by the staff. After a few repeats of this, the staff simply gave up and allowed the old men to hover outside where they strained to hear every sound coming from inside the room.

Finally, when they were on yet another slow lap of the vast mansion, they could hear footsteps approaching behind them. It was the doctor. Lucien froze as a cold chill flooded through him. Memories of Lillian came flooding through as he watched the doctor walk down the long corridor. He felt

as though his heart was going to stop beating there and then. But the doctor was smiling broadly and there was no visible signs of concern in his step. Lucien still needed to hear him say the words. He would not be right until then.

"Congratulations," the doctor beamed.

He was fully aware of what had happened to Lucien's daughter in childbirth so he got directly to the point.

"Both mother and baby are doing great. There were no complications whatsoever. Mabel is tired and a little sore but very well and tremendously happy."

Lucien had to grasp onto Crusher for support such was the effect of the surge of relief that coursed through his body. The doctor laughed as he watched the two old men embrace each other affectionately, if not a little stiffly.

"You're sure, doctor?" Lucien asked, needing further reassurance.

"Absolutely. Mabel is sitting up and ready for visitors to see her beautiful and perfectly formed daughter."

It was only then that Lucien realized that he hadn't asked whether it was a boy or a girl.

"Another girl," he complained to Crusher. "Why do the women in this family object to having boys?"

He was kidding, of course, right at that moment, he was beyond happy. He had lost Evangeline and Lillian and he knew his heart wouldn't be able to stand it, if something had happened to Mabel.

The doctor coughed and started to say, "There's just one thing."

Before he could continue, Lucien rounded on him aggressively, "But you said they were fine. What one thing? What?"

"Believe me, they are fine. They are both doing really well. It's just…"

His voice tailed off. Lucien and Crusher stared at him expectantly.

"Just what?" Lucien asked in complete exasperation. "Spit it out, man, for God's sake."

The doctor had a change of heart. He put his professional face on and smiled at them.

"It's nothing. They're waiting for you. Go see them."

Lucien looked at the doctor for a long moment, then he and Crusher strode to Mabel's bedroom. She was sitting up waiting for them, baby in her arms, looking so beautiful and happy. Then Lucien realized what the doctor had started to tell them; behind him, he heard Crusher exclaim, "Holy shit!"

There was no mystery now about what race the father of Mabel's baby had been. In her arms, lay this tiny baby with a mass of black hair and beautiful coffee-colored skin. Lucien could tell that Mabel was looking at him a little nervously, trying to gauge his reaction. But Lucien had truly learned from his daughter and all he saw there lying in the bed was his family, his granddaughter and great-granddaughter alive and well. For Lucien Cartwright, that was all that mattered. Everything else were details. Unimportant details.

"Oh Mabel, she's beautiful. I am so proud of you. Can I hold her?"

Mabel's eyes filled with tears, even Crusher sniffled in the background as she handed the baby over to her grandfather.

"I'm going to name her Bella," she informed him.

Lucien looked lovingly at the sleeping baby in his arms.

"Bella. That's a great name. Bella the beautiful. Bella the beautiful."

That night, Lucien wrote Hank Holder once more and extended another invitation for him to come visit. He informed Hank about Bella and told him that Mabel was doing great.

"We would greatly welcome your presence here, Hank," the letter continued.

"After the tragedy that accompanied the last birth in our family, this is a truly joyful even and we are certainly blessed. I now believe this is the time for our family to be united and I urge you, respectfully, to come see your beautiful daughter and granddaughter."

Two weeks later, Hank's response came in the mail. Once again, he thanked Lucien for bringing him up to date on events in the family and emphasized how much he appreciated receiving yet another invitation to come visit.

"Yet, I must respectfully once more decline. I am sure you will be surprised by this and perhaps you won't understand but it is my belief that the time is not yet right. Once again, I feel certain that when that time does arrive then I will be there. I trust you will not take offence at this position of mine, for none is surely intended. Please give my love to Mabel and a kiss to Bella for me."

Lucien stared at the letter for a long time.

"You're absolutely right, Hank, I don't understand but I will not criticize or second guess you. I just hope I'll still be alive when you believe the time is right, that's all."

Once again, he had broken the news to Mabel and once again, she put on a brave face.

"Then we'll just have to wait for him, won't we, little one?" she said as she held Bella in her arms. "We'll just wait here until he's ready."

Chapter Twenty

1964
Strongville, Georgia

Baby Bella had just turned three months old. She was a chubby, happy baby who just seemed to smile all the time and she was totally doted upon.

"It's gas, Gramps," Mabel said for the umpteenth time after her grandfather had once more commented how Bella always smiled at him.

"Maybe she just likes me," he retorted. "Did you ever stop to consider that fact?"

"Oh, I'm sure she likes you, Gramps. Why wouldn't she? You spoil her so much. But that smile right there. That'd be gas."

And so it went on. The house had settled into a comfortable and happy routine all centered on Bella and her needs. It seemed to Mabel that Crusher Conway had all but moved in, he was there so often and it amused her no end to see the big tough former sheriff cooing with delight at the little dark-skinned baby in his arms.

Truly one for the books, she would think to herself.

One afternoon, when Bella was down for a nap, Mabel entered the study where her grandfather and Crusher were engaged in their daily battle of wills over the chessboard.

"Hey there, young lady," Crusher called out when she entered. "Want to come watch me whup your granddaddy's butt? I'm about to do so."

Lucien snorted derisively.

"Listen to him and his big talk with me just two moves away from checkmating him."

Before Crusher could respond with a cutting retort, Mabel interjected, "Well, I do thank you kindly gentlemen for what has to be the most intriguing offer I received all week, but I'm actually here on another matter."

Lucien looked at her, studying her face for any telltale signs of worry or anything that might be a cause for concern. Seeing none, he said, "Well, speak your mind, dear, the floor is yours."

Mabel hesitated and sensing her nerve beginning to falter, came right out with it.

"So, Gramps, would be it okay if I went away for a few days?"

The instant look of horror on both men's faces made her continue immediately, "It would be just me by myself. I was hoping to leave Bella with you both and the nanny."

She actually didn't know right then whether she should be amused or insulted by the relief that flooded their faces. Lucien thought for a moment and in a measured tone replied, "Well, I don't see why not. Might one enquire where it is you're planning to go?"

Mabel looked at him, this was going to be the difficult part. She was tempted to lie and say she was going to visit

a friend for a few days but she respected Lucien too much to do that and, besides, he might be old but her grandfather was as sharp as a tack and could smell a rat a mile away. So, she took a deep breath and said, "I'm going to Sterling, Mississippi. Just for three days. No longer."

"Sterling, Mississippi," Lucien repeated. "And might one also enquire what would entice you to go there?"

Before she could respond, Crusher spoke up, "I can answer that. There's going to be some kind of a civil rights gathering there this week. That's why you're going there. Am I right?"

"Yes, kind of. It's more of a meeting, and a very small one at that. There won't be much going on."

But Crusher wasn't buying that story.

"That's not the way I hear it. I understand some high-ranking folks in the civil rights movement are going to gather in Sterling and there's talk of trouble. Folks down there won't appreciate what they see as out of state agitators arriving on their doorstep and stirring things up."

He turned to Lucien.

"It ain't my call, Lucien, but I'm not in favor of this. There's a lot of good old boys in that part of the world who'd happily take the law into their own hands to protect what they see as their rights. They won't care if you're black or white, if you get in their way."

"Oh, hush now, Crusher," Mabel admonished. "You know that's an exaggeration. It's just a little gathering, Gramps. There won't be any trouble. I'll only be gone for three days and besides it'll give you boys to spoil Bella even more than you do when I'm around."

Lucien was torn. He shared Crusher's concerns but he didn't want to put boundaries around Mabel that she might rebel against. Crusher, for his part, wasn't finished.

"Okay, Mabel, how about I come with you and keep out for you?"

Mabel put her hands on her hips, tilted her head, and said, "I appreciate the offer, I really do but with all due respect, I'm not convinced that this gathering is one you need to attend. No offense."

"I didn't mean go to the meeting," Crusher declared, shaking his head in exasperation. "I know I wouldn't be welcome. I just meant that I'd tag along for the ride and stay out of the way when we get to Sterling. You'll never even notice I'm there."

Mabel shook her head again.

"Thanks Crusher, but no. Some time alone will do me good and I'll be home in three days. Gramps, please."

Lucien knew well that Mabel was just being respectful asking his permission and he appreciated that. Despite his misgivings, he nodded but added, "Promise you'll call when you get there and when you're leaving to come home."

"I promise," she replied and gave him a hug.

Crusher to his credit was one persistent animal when he wanted to be.

"Look Mabel, I'm not passing judgement on this cause and God knows it's not like change isn't needed but you've got a young baby to look after, isn't your place with her?"

Mabel knew his heart was in the right place and that his objections were simply out of concern for her safety, so she merely hugged him too and said, "Three days. No more.

118

Now you promise that you won't have ruined her completely by the time I return."

The next morning, she set off for Mississippi. It had been really hard to leave Bella but she knew the baby was in good hands and would be lavished with love and attention the whole time she was gone. Lucien watched her car disappear down the driveway. He would worry every moment until she returned.

But Mabel never returned home. She had phoned to say that she had arrived safely and that was the last that was heard from her. When there was no phone call after four, five then six days, Lucien knew something was terribly wrong.

Crusher used his contacts in law enforcement to make enquiries but he was stonewalled. He didn't want to contact the sheriff directly so he used intermediaries who all reported back that they believed something had happened and was being covered up. It was only when Lucien used his influence with state officials that the story began to emerge that three young people had gone missing: two black males from New York and a white girl from Georgia.

Lucien kept pushing for answers and after two weeks, three bodies were pulled out of the river. They were chained together and a weight had been attached before they were thrown off a bridge just outside of town. An autopsy showed that they had been alive when they entered the water. The local sheriff's department looked into the incident but concluded there was insufficient evidence that a crime had been committed.

The Federal government declined to investigate. The case was closed. Meanwhile, Crusher's contacts reported

back that two white residents were bragging around town how they had sent a message to any niggers or nigger lovers about interfering in their business.

Lucien was rocked to his core. He had lost Evangeline and that had been tragic but her passing was the natural cycle of life, so he had accepted it. Then Lillian was taken from him at such a young age and now Mabel at an even younger age. He couldn't take anymore.

The joy and vigor that he had shown after Bella's birth evaporated out of him leaving only a hollow shrunken skeletal frame with eyes that just stared unseeingly into space. Crusher Conway was heartbroken also but now he was extremely worried about Lucien's health. There was no way Lucien could go and reclaim Mabel's body but he didn't feel comfortable going to Sterling himself and leaving Lucien behind. So, he organized for Mabel's body to be transported home and set about making arrangements for the funeral.

Hank Holder received a third letter from Georgia. This time from Crusher. The letter simply stated the facts; Mabel had been murdered, drowned deliberately for believing in a change for the good. The letter went on to say when the funeral was going to be held. There was no invitation to come visit on this occasion. Crusher knew that Hank would come now upon hearing this news.

Crusher was right. Hank finally traveled back to Georgia. He had squandered the opportunity to see his daughter alive and he would carry the shame of that for the rest of his but he would be there for her funeral. He had always believed that seeing Mabel would have brought back so many painful memories of Lillian that it would send him

spiraling back into the abyss. He cursed himself for being so weak, so selfish. He was determined not to repeat the error with his granddaughter.

The reunion of Hank and Lucien was both tender and heartbreaking. There was no stiff, uncomfortable handshake this time as there had been in Chicago many years ago. The two men simply hugged each other tightly for a long time, each of them wrapped in their own memories and in their own grief. Even Crusher Conway came and hugged him. Hank had to admit that surprised him, but in a good way.

Mabel's funeral was held on a Saturday afternoon. At first, the rector was reluctant to hold the ceremony in the whites only church but relented after Crusher leaned on him hard. The rector knew this would be an unpopular move with the majority of white folk who considered Lucien a traitor to their race.

They knew by now that Hank Holder was Mabel's father, they knew that Bella had a black father, and that Mabel had perished agitating with black folk in Mississippi. That was too much for them to accept so they boycotted the funeral to the point where only twelve white mourners turned up.

On the other hand, the black community rallied behind Hank and the Cartwright's and they thronged the church, taking every available seat and standing space. Lucien was very touched and he felt that, at least, some good had come from his family's efforts these past few years.

Hank sat in the front row seat between Lucien and Crusher. He listened to the preacher speak about Mabel but it seemed to Hank that he was only going through the motions. But it was the surprising eloquence of Crusher

Conway's elegy that had the complete congregation in tears. That this gruff, no nonsense former sheriff could describe Mabel in such thoughtful manner with words that flowed directly from his heart, shocked everyone.

Every now and then, Crusher would have to stop, wipe his tears away, and gather himself before he could continue. His emotions, raw and unchecked, filled the church with a sadness that lay heavy in the air until they landed on those sitting there listening and bound their sorrow together.

The local black choir sang several hymns and a soloist gave a rendition of Amazing Grace that few who were present that day would ever forget. For Lucien it finally became clear what Mabel had always known, her home was with the black community, this was where she belonged. And on that day, in that church, he reached a decision that would change the history of his family forever.

Lucien had invited those who attended the funeral to come back to the Cartwright mansion for food and drink. He had taken the time to tell the catering company to send only white staff. This was not a totally unusual request as often white people just didn't want blacks preparing or serving food in their houses.

It was a complete surprise, and not a pleasant one at that, when the wait staff learned that the request was not because of the sensibilities of whites but because Lucien did not want to offend his black guests by having black people wait on them in a house that had one time owned slaves. Apart from Lucien, the only white face at the house apart from the wait staff, was Crusher Conway and that suited Lucien fine.

Later that night, Lucien asked Hank to sit with him on the porch. He fetched a bottle of his best bourbon and two

glasses. They sat in silence at first sipping their drinks, listening to the sounds of the farm. Then Lucien turned to Hank.

"Forgive me, Hank, but I'm going to jump right in here. I don't have much left in me. I fought back after Lillian died but I can't do it again. The will is gone. All gone."

He continued, "You remember Hank in the hospital in Chicago, you asked me to take Mabel, bring her back here, and raise her. You said that it wouldn't work for a single black man trying to bring up a girl who looked white. A better life, was what you said I could give her."

Lucien stopped and let his words linger in the evening air.

"Maybe that was right but maybe it was wrong. I honestly think that Mabel was only happy the last year of her life, while she was pregnant and after Bella was born. Would she only have been happy for one year with you? I can't answer that and neither can you."

"I can answer it, Lucien," said Hank forcefully. "I was in no fit state to bring that child up and I know you know that because it was you who kept me from falling too far. For that I'll always be grateful. The person that Mabel became, that beautiful, caring human being was all down to you and Evangeline. Don't ever sell yourself short on that score."

"Be that as it may," replied Lucien, "and I thank you for saying it, we really don't know. But what we do know is that Bella must be with you now. I'd like you to come here and live with us for as long as I have left. After I pass, you'll get the house and the land and you can in turn leave it to

Bella. What do you say? It makes the most sense, doesn't it?"

As Hank sat there listening to Lucien, he briefly entertained the prospect of Lucien's request, then he shook his head and said:

"No, Lucien. I won't come and live here but I will take Bella with me and raise her in Kentucky. You put the money and the land in some trust for her where she gets it when she's old enough. I won't take your money but I do ask that you make enough available to me so that Bella can get the finest education possible. I don't want her to lose out on any one single chance in life because the color of her skin denied her the best education possible. If you can agree to this, we have a deal."

Lucien had known this would be Hank's response. He never expected Hank to agree to live in the Cartwright family home. Yet as he despaired of losing Bella, he didn't want her to be here and witness him fading away into the nothingness his grief was pulling him towards. He made up his mind and as he spoke the words, the white, southern, slave owning Cartwright lineage would forever more be black.

"We have a deal, Hank. We have a deal."

"That's good, Lucien. I need two to three days to clear up some things so I'll head out in the morning and I'll come back to get Mabel when I'm done."

"Anything I can help with you with?" Lucien asked.

"No, sir," he said, standing up. "I'll bid you good night now."

"Goodnight, Hank," Lucien said. "I'll stop here a while and finish my drink."

Lucien sat there thinking, then he went inside to make a phone call.

Chapter Twenty-One
1964
Strongville, Georgia

The next morning, Hank set out a little after ten. When he reached the end of the driveway, he saw that the exit was blocked. Crusher Conway had parked his truck across the driveway making it impossible for Hank to pass. He was leaning casually against the truck, smoking.

"Excuse me, sheriff," Hank said after he had rolled down his window, "can I get by you? I need to leave."

Crusher continued to smoke before replying, "Well now, I can't rightly do that, Hank."

"Why not, sheriff, I don't understand?"

"I tell you what, Hank, why don't you come out and we'll talk?"

Hank wasn't sure whether he should be worried or not. Crusher didn't seem like he had a problem with him but he just understand what was going on.

"You see, Hank, here's my problem. I know where you're going and I know what you're aiming to do."

"And what's that, sheriff?" asked Hank rather defensively.

"You're going to Sterling, Mississippi, to take care of those crackers who killed Mabel just as you took care of Billy Ray and those other fools years ago."

Like everyone else by now, Hank had heard the stories of the white men in Sterling bragging about killing Mabel and her two companions.

"I thought I wasn't wanted for any crime in the State of Georgia?" Hank challenged Crusher.

"Oh, you're not, Hank; you most certainly are not. All I'm trying to say is if you intend to go to Sterling Mississippi to take care of those boys then the only way it's going to happen is if I come too. I tried to persuade Mabel to let me go with her and she wouldn't. I blame myself for not going anyway and I'll be goddamned if I'm going let you go and get yourself killed also."

Crusher stared at him with an unmovable expression hardened on his face. Hank knew he was defeated. Besides he was older now and he could use the help against younger men. He nodded at Crusher.

"Good. At least you're seeing sense. Drive your car back up to the house and we'll go in my truck."

On the journey to Sterling, Crusher told Hank what his plan was. He would drop Hank off at the bridge on the outskirts of town where the crime was committed. Then he was going to drive into town and talk to the sheriff. He would pretend that he was the big, racist former sheriff who had come all the way from Georgia to Sterling because he was so impressed at the decisive way they had taken care of a nigger problem. He would then get the sheriff to introduce him to the perpetrators, get them drunk, and lure them out to the bridge where Hank would be waiting.

"It's a little rusty right now," Crusher admitted. "But we'll refine it as we go along."

He dropped Hank off at the bridge, warned him to stay out of sight and took off for town. Surprisingly, the plan worked perfectly. The sheriff in Sterling was tickled pink that a fellow lawman had seen fit to travel all the way from Georgia to express his admiration for how he ran his town. Crusher had laid it on thick and heavy and the sheriff swallowed it whole.

He brought Crusher to meet the two men who had murdered Mabel. It was all Crusher could do not to shoot them there and then but he and Hank had other plans for them so he sat and bought them beer after and beer and listened to stories that made his skin crawl. Finally, he said, "Hey boys, I brought me this camera and I'd sure appreciate it if y'all would take a picture of me on the bridge where nothing happened, if you get my drift."

The two men were after several beers by now and since the sheriff had introduced Crusher as a friend, they had put their guard down completely. So, they all piled into Crusher's truck and headed to the bridge. Crusher made a big show of preparing his camera and when their backs were turned, he came up behind them and put a gun on the back of each of their heads.

"Are you there, Hank?" he called out as the two men froze. "Listen to me, motherfuckers, one move and I'll blow your fucking brains out."

Hank arrived out of the shadows carrying chains and a twenty pound weight. He silently proceeded to wrap the chain around the by now petrified men and finally attached the weight. They lifted the men up on to the rail and left

them sit there for a moment. The men were howling by now but there was nobody to hear them.

Crusher looked them in the eye and said, "You killed what was most precious to the two of us. Now it's your turn."

With that he pushed them over the edge into the water where they quickly disappeared from sight.

"Let's go," he said, "before someone sees us."

The drive back was mostly in silence. Hank asked Crusher once if he was worried that the sheriff might come after him. Crusher had laughed.

"That chicken shit. He's just a coward with a badge. No way he's coming after me."

It was almost morning when Crusher dropped Hank off at the Cartwright farm. Lucien heard Hank come in. He knew it had been taken care of and he was pleased.

The next day, Hank and Bella left for Kentucky. Neither of them would ever see Lucien and Crusher alive again.

Chapter Twenty-Two
June 1982
Edgarville, Kentucky

Hank had not been able concentrate on his work or even sit still for one moment today. His stomach was in knots. Today was graduation day at Briar Run High School and his granddaughter, his own precious Bella, was not only graduating but she was doing so first in her class and had been chosen class valedictorian. Tonight, the beautiful young lady that he had picked up and moved to Kentucky when she was just a baby and lovingly reared all by himself, was going to stand in front of an audience of many hundred and give this year's commencement speech.

Hank was proud beyond description and similarly nervous in equal parts. Although Briar Run High School had been fully integrated for a number of decades by now, tonight would mark the very first occasion when it had a black valedictorian making a speech at the graduation ceremony.

When Bella had told him one evening after he had returned from work, Hank had taken her face in his hands,

looked her steadily in the eye, and, choking back the tears, counseled her.

"This is a huge honor, Bella, and one you truly deserve. When you get up on the stage to make that speech, don't act like you're apologizing for anything and don't come across like you're bragging about being there. Be your own natural self and remember you come from a long line of strong and extraordinary women. Your blessed mom; your grandma, Lillian; and your great grandma, Evangeline. These were all women who faced the biggest of challenges and who met them head on. They would each be so proud of you, as I am."

"Why, grandpa," Bella teased, "maybe I should get you to write my speech. You have such a way with words."

And she had worked so hard on her speech, parsing each and every word over and over again. Hank could hear late at night, pacing her bedroom floor practicing over and over again.

Now finally here he was sitting in the school hall waiting for the ceremony to commence. The place was packed and it was hot and stuffy. Hank tugged incessantly at the stiff collar on his best shirt and longed to loosen his tie but he dared not. As proud as he was of Bella, he was also sad that he was the only family member she had, so there would be no-one else present to share this historic moment with.

Bella's mother, Mabel, had gone to her grave with the identity of who her father was and her great grandfather, Lucien, had passed away almost sixteen years ago. Even Crusher Conway, the onetime bigoted sheriff of Strongville, who had become so close to Mabel and Bella, he had finally

succumbed to the lung cancer brought about by his long years of chain smoking. No, it would just be Hank in the audience tonight just as it had been for the vast majority of Bella's life.

At eighteen, Bella had never even met an aunt, uncle, or cousin of hers. Hank had never traveled back to Georgia and he had lost contact over the years with his own family. Every Christmas, every Thanksgiving, it had just been two of them. Hank had had a major crash course in on-the-job training about how to rear a little girl. He had been thrown in at the deep end with no experience and no support. He thought back to all the challenges he had overcome. No, he corrected himself almost immediately, that they had overcome together.

Whereas he had learned from Lucien that Mabel had been wild and difficult, Bella had been an absolute pleasure to rear. It was, he thought, as if she sensed from a young age that he couldn't do it all by himself and that she had a role to play also. So, piece by piece, they figured it out together. Even the sensitive female issues that arrived as she got older, were tackled in an open and cooperative manner.

For her part, Bella had believed that the cooperative parenting model they had adopted had to her being mature beyond her years and given her the leadership skills her classmates and teachers had all acknowledged.

As the parade of graduates began, Hank turned in his seat to catch a glimpse of Bella walking through the hall with her fellow graduates. He knew she wouldn't be hard to spot. Bella had grown to five feet ten and with her unruly mass of curly hair coupled with the added inches her shoes gave her, she would stand out in the crowd. As she passed

by, she turned, flashed him a mischievous grin then kept going.

He was so proud of her. He had thought it was completely ironic that Bella, with all the money in the world from great grandfather available to her to spend on her education, had received countless offers of academic and sporting scholarships. Having reviewed each offer in detail and weighed up all of the pros and cons, Bella had decided to turn down each and every scholarship and pay her own way.

She had finally decided upon Harvard, which was also one of the schools that had offered her a scholarship, and wasn't really surprised when her application had been quickly accepted. If the Admissions Officer in Harvard thought it strange that a young black student from Kentucky would turn down a full-ride scholarship and choose to pay full freight, he never once questioned it.

From Bella's perspective, paying her own way meant that she would neither be beholden to anyone nor would she feel like she was denying a scholarship opportunity to a less fortunate student. This was what the family money was there for and she considered her decision to go to Harvard and study law a very worthwhile investment. While Bella knew from Hank that there was old family money in trust for her until she reached twenty-five, she had no idea how wealth she actually was. Hank thought it preferable that it way. In addition, they had kept the family estate in Strongville, which was now being run by a manager and which would also become Bella's when she turned twenty-five.

To Hank, the ceremony both dragged on interminably and flew by far too quickly. He wanted to see and hear Bella but he was also dreading it. She had the weight of history on her young shoulders and it was a big burden to bear. At last, the principal was introducing Bella; lauding her for all her sporting and academic achievements, proudly stating that she was heading to Harvard and commending her for the wonderful young lady she had become.

Then Bella walked to the podium and looked out at the assembled crowd. She knew there were many in the audience who were not happy with her being chosen to give this speech. She also knew that this list included parents of students, staff members and even her own classmates. As she stood there, she knew she had to get this right and she thought of Hank's advice not to be apologetic or boastful. She began to speak.

"Good evening, my name is Bella Cartwright Holder and it is an honor and privilege to speak to you tonight. I would first like to thank all those who made it possible for me to have this opportunity to stand in front of you tonight on behalf of the wonderful class of 1982."

She paused for a moment as her eyes found Hank. He was sitting there as stiff as a board with a look of sheer terror on his face. Their eyes met and she winked at him. It was one of the most touching moments of his whole life. There, standing on that stage, faced with the biggest task of her whole life to date, Bella had taken a moment to wink at an old man. If he hadn't been already overcome with tears, Hank would have certainly started right there and then. She broke eye contact with Hank and turned to the audience.

"I would like to speak to you about a journey. After all, those of us graduating here tonight will now commence a new and exciting journey in this next chapter of your lives. But that's not the journey I wish to speak about. That story has yet to be written so it will fall to another speaker at another time to recount those tales. No, I want to speak about journeys that have either been fully completed or are underway, the journeys that have led each and every one of us to this very room, on this very night.

"And I believe, if we traced the history of each individual journey that led here tonight, we would find the history of our country traced alongside it, matching it and mirroring along the way. If then we looked back with closer inspection, there on the path to this hall where we have assembled tonight, we would see the many challenges that were faced, battles that were fought, victories gained and defeats endured.

"We would see great moments of enlightenment where we shone like the brightest lighthouse and dark passages of time that brought shame, guilt and suffering. We would see courage, daring, fear and resolve. There would be moments when the sense of community and inclusion were a beauty and wonder to behold and times when we looked at our neighbors as if they were enemies and tried to defeat them. Those are the stories of each of us, of each of our families and they mirror the story of our country, that tonight we should be so proud of, so grateful to for this opportunity it has given us."

Bella looked at the audience. She had their attention. She could see expressions that were genuinely interested and curious, worried expressions that she might pick open

135

still festering sores and expressions of open hostility. She hoped that by the end of her speech she would not have added to any divisions but rather had helped to bring her classmates and her community together. This, she knew perfectly well, was a tall order indeed and she worried whether she might just be too young for the task.

It was time to make her speech personal. Time to reveal to the audience, her family history and secrets that not been openly shared before. It was her goal, by doing so, to make people try to understand that how really wrong it can be to draw conclusions without understanding all of the facts.

"And so it is with my own history and my personal journey to be here with you tonight. People will say, and with justification, that for Bella Cartwright Holder to be standing here tonight speaking to this audience is a great step forward in the journey of our wonderful country. And yes, it is.

"I know my grandfather, Hank, is sitting there among you feeling very proud of his granddaughter. But in the history of my family, my standing here tonight is not that unusual or special. For both my grandmother and great grandmother were also class valedictorians and had the privilege of making their class graduation speech also at fine southern institutions, such as our own school."

Bella paused as she heard the audible gasp and she could sense the audience attempting to process her words and understand them. She could see the puzzled faces as they tried to work it out in their minds. She could almost read their minds.

"What is this black girl saying?" Or "Listen to that crazy nigger."

Bella was almost sure she could tell who phrased the question what way purely by the looks on the faces of the people in the audience. But they were all thinking exactly the same; fifty or seventy years ago, there were no class valedictorians or graduation speeches made by colored girls, here in Dixie.

Bella waited a few seconds longer to let what she had said sink in before continuing.

"During the First World War, in nineteen seventeen, my great grandmother Evangeline Cartwright, or Evangeline Cooper as she was then, gave the graduation speech at one of the most prestigious girls academies in Atlanta, Georgia; Miss Copeland's School for Young Ladies."

Bella could now very clearly see the effect her words were having on the audience. That she was standing there, as a young black woman, declaring that her great grandmother had attended an upper-class white only school in the South was deeply shocking.

"Curiously enough, when the Second World War was raging, my grandmother Lillian Cartwright, also had the privilege of making her own graduation speech at the same school. Unfortunately, my own mother, Mabel Cartwright, died before she had the opportunity to graduate high school but there is no doubt in my mind, however, that if she had been allowed to live, she too would have carried on the tradition of the Cartwright women.

"As it happens, my mother Mabel, lost her life in Sterling, Mississippi, when she and two companions were bound together by chains and thrown alive off a bridge with a weight attached to them. They were killed because they believed in a better life for each citizen of this country.

"A simple belief but one my mother was ready to die for her. Mabel Cartwright, didn't get to make a graduation speech but the statement of her actions was far more profound than any words spoken by Cartwright women before or after her."

Now you could have heard a pin drop in the hall. No one seemed to even take a breath. If she had thrown them for a loop with her story about her great grandmother and grandmother, the bombshell tale of the circumstances surrounding her mother's death hit the hall hard. It was time now to take another turn.

"I said at the beginning that each of our stories mirror the history of our country and I have tried to show you how mine does. But for all its complexity and challenges, my story is simply at its core, a love story. Yes, a truly wonderful love story. And isn't that the story of our country too? A love story. The bonds between a land and its people, between ideals and aspirations and the ultimate will to be free. Isn't that what makes us love this great land of ours through the good times, the bad times and the downright ugly times."

Bella looked at the audience, this was not the speech they had anticipated and definitely not the speech they had wanted to hear tonight. But she could see tear-stained faces, hands reaching out to hold the hand next to them and she knew she had touched them but she wasn't done, not yet.

"My own love story is a very simple one and one that I know will match many of your own stories. A boy goes off to war to fight for his country, he comes home a man, meets a girl, falls in love and they have a baby. Yes, I'm absolutely

sure this story has been repeated countless times through many wars.

"In my case, though, the love was forbidden, it was impossible. The girl was white, beautiful and rich. The boy was black and poor. And it was through the very impossibility of this forbidden love, through its strength and deep commitment that lives were changed. Old ways were put aside, differences were seen as just that and not viewed as better or worse.

"This boy and this girl, with their love, changed the lives of many people and put me here tonight. This country, with its love and its strength, has also changed the lives of so many people and put me, Bella Cartwright Holder, standing here in front of you tonight. And I am here tonight, neither black nor white but American and so very proud to be one.

"Thank you for listening to me tell my story. I hope we can all go forward with love and strength for each other and for this country. God bless you all and thank you."

It was done, she had made the speech that she had agonized so much over. She wondered if she would get into trouble. She wondered if there would be a backlash. Bella stood there and wondered why in the seconds after she had finished the hall was still completely silent. As the silence continued, she could feel a knot growing in her stomach and she wanted to run off the stage. She had blown it. They had hated it. She had ruined everything.

The silence persisted several more agonizing seconds until suddenly, the audience erupted as if they had collectively emerged from a trance at the very same time. Through her own tears she could see they were on their feet

clapping and cheering. The principal and staff members walked over to her and hugged her, her classmates jumped up and down shouting her name. Finally, the principal put his arm around her and spoke into the microphone, "I am the principal and these are the staff of Briar Run High School."

He gestured towards all the teachers who had by now assembled at the podium.

"And this young lady is our pupil. Thank you so much, Bella Cartwright Holder, no one who had the privilege to be here tonight will ever, ever, ever forget your words."

Bella stood there, emotionally overwrought. She was glad the principal still had his arm around her for she could feel her knees begin to buckle and her legs give way. As she watched and listened, it felt to Bella that she now could stand alongside the Cartwright women who had gone before her and who had demonstrated their courage and their strength when they were most needed. But most especially, this was for her grandfather who she knew would truly understand the enormity of what had just taken place.

Hank had sat there listening to Bella weave the story of their family in to a beautiful and emotional narrative. He was extremely touched by her comments about Mabel, the mother she never knew and the daughter he had never seen alive. He thought back to Lillian and how proud she would have been at the way her granddaughter, with grace, poise and a maturity beyond her years, had delivered a speech that was as soul searching as it was uplifting.

Throughout the speech, the one abiding thought in Hank's mind that was that Bella was now all grown up and would be heading to Harvard soon. That was the worst part.

He would be all alone, again, and he dreaded the prospect of it. He shook himself. This was Bella's night. He wasn't going to allow anything to detract from that. He couldn't wait to hug her and tell her what a great job she had done.

Chapter Twenty-Three
April 1989
Edgarville, Kentucky

"Dinner, Friday night?" Hank asked when they were sitting chatting in the sunshine after Finn had completed his morning run.

"Absolutely, my friend."

They had been meeting for dinner twice a week since the beginning of the year and their friendship had deepened to the point where they had each revealed long kept secrets about events in their respective lives. On every occasion, they had met at Finn's apartment where they ate pizza and drank beer. Finn couldn't help but stare at Hank in amazement then when he heard the older man say.

"My place all right with you? Say around seven-thirtyish."

Finn, momentarily dumbfounded, just nodded while Hank told him the address.

That Friday night, Finn left his apartment at seven. It was about a twenty-minute walk to Hank's home and he planned to pick up some beer along the way. He wondered if Hank had a porch or a deck. It was a very warm evening,

perfect for sitting outside, drinking beer, and having a good chat.

When he arrived at the address Hank had given him, Finn stopped to admire the nicely painted home and it's meticulously maintained lawn. He knew Hank really enjoyed working with his hands, especially outdoors, so he wasn't at all surprised at what he saw. He was also happy to see that Hank did indeed have a porch with some very comfortable looking chairs.

Finn rang the doorbell and waited. He had turned around to look once more at the brightly colored flowers and shrubs in the lawn when he heard the door open.

"I really like your…"

Finn started to say but his voice tailed off almost immediately. It wasn't Hank who had opened the door as Finn had been expecting. Instead, standing there was a tall and stunningly beautiful woman of about twenty-five or twenty-six. She was wearing a short, black, sleeveless dress that showed off toned arms and perfectly formed legs that seemed to extend forever until they reached smart-looking black pumps. They stared at each other for a few seconds until Finn realized that she was waiting for him to speak said.

"Hi, I'm Finn. Is Hank around? He invited me over for dinner."

Then, because he was somehow becoming nervous by the woman's frank stare, he added lamely, "I brought beer."

Then he lifted the beer up to show it to her, in case for some reason she might not have understood. He immediately cursed himself for being such an idiot.

"So I see," the young woman replied solemnly as if Finn had revealed a great secret to her.

If Finn was surprised to see a woman standing in the doorway of Hank's house, then Bella was even more shocked to see him there. She knew that Hank had developed a friendship with someone he had met in the park where he worked but she had assumed that it was a person his own age and black. The last thing she had expected to see standing on her doorstep was an extremely attractive, extremely fit-looking, young white man, with a funny accent to boot. She regained her composure.

"Hi, I'm Bella. Hank's granddaughter. I live here with him."

Now Finn was truly stunned. As close as he and Hank had grown and as much they had told each other, there had never been any mention of a granddaughter and certainly not one who lived with him.

They stood a few more moments in silence just looking at each other, both of them lost in their own thoughts as they tried to process this unexpected development. Bella broke the spell first.

"I'm so sorry, where are my manners? Please come in and bring that beer you're so proud of with you."

She added the last part of that sentence with a mischievous grin growing on her perfectly formed lips beneath which straight, even white teeth glowed. Finn blushed and replied sheepishly, "Sorry, I guess I was a little taken aback. I had assumed that Hank lived by himself."

"I think we both got a surprise there."

"Well, I think you're still ahead of me. At least you were expecting someone for dinner."

Bella faced him and looked him straight in the eye.

"Yes, that's true but to be perfectly honest, I was not expecting you."

"Then I'm sorry to disappoint you."

Bella flashed that mischievous grin once more.

"I never said I was disappointed now, did I? Anyway, I'll let grandpa know you're here."

She stood at the bottom of the stairway and shouted up to Hank.

"Grandpa, your guest is here."

Finn could have sworn she had placed a sarcastic emphasis on the word 'guest' but Bella's look was all innocence. They heard Hank's voice in response.

"Thanks Bella. Glad you could make it, Finn. I'll be down presently."

Bella turned to Finn.

"Do you want to come into the kitchen? I'm still working on dinner and we can have a drink of that famous beer while we're waiting or I have wine also, if you'd like that instead."

Another surprise, Finn had been sure that dinner would have been their usual menu of pizza and beer. Now Hank's previously unknown granddaughter was talking about cooking and offering wine. He followed Bella into the kitchen, where clearly something extremely appetizing was cooking.

"Wow, something sure smells good. What is it?"

There went that grin again and Bella almost laughed out loud as she replied.

"Well, in keeping with tonight's theme, it's a surprise. You'll just have to wait and see. Now wine or beer?"

Finn laughed. He was already enjoying Bella's quick wit and he knew he'd have to stay on his toes if he was going to match her.

"Beer, please. I wonder why Hank was so secretive about you and about me as well?"

"Perhaps, he was embarrassed or ashamed of something or someone?"

Finn waited a moment then deadpanned.

"Hmm, perhaps. Understandably so."

Bella was not to be outdone easily though.

"Yes, after twenty-six years of living with me, he knows how high my standards are."

"Ouch," Finn replied, touching his heart. "Don't pull your punches anyway."

After Hank had replied to Bella that he'd join them shortly, he sat in his favorite chair and picked up the book he was reading. He glanced at the clock on the dresser, chuckled softly.

"I'll give them about thirty minutes to get acquainted, then I'll join them."

He had told Finn to arrive at seven thirty and Bella that dinner was going to be at eight. He picked up his book and began to read.

Downstairs in the kitchen, Finn and Bella were getting on like a house on fire. She had enquired about his funny accent and how come he had ended up here in Edgarville of all places. In return, he had asked her about what she did for a living. The conversation flowed easily back and forth between them.

Finn learned that Bella had graduated first in her law class at Harvard and though she had plenty of offers from

prestigious firms, many of whom would have been delighted to employ such a highly accomplished black woman, she had turned them all down to return back home to Edgarville. She now worked for a small, minority law firm that exclusively took on cases of discrimination and racial abuse; often for little or no fees.

Finn was very impressed at her selflessness. To turn down such impressive offers and career advancement opportunities to return home and try to right wrongs was a big sacrifice. He admired her greatly for that.

They chatted back and forth, enjoying both each other's company and the opportunity to test the other's wit and quickness of thought. Neither of them seemed to notice that Hank was taking an inordinately long time to join them.

Hank could hear the constant sound of their voices and the flow of their conversation. He had thought long and hard about this. He loved Bella more than anything else in the world but he worried about her. She had always been popular with lots of friends but she never had a boyfriend. She had turned down offers to go to prom and all through college she had focused exclusively on her studies and her athletics. She didn't go to parties or do any of the wild things he had heard that college kids did.

On one hand, he was very grateful for that, her mother had gotten pregnant at seventeen and he didn't Bella going that route, on the other hand, she was too serious for her own good. He was constantly on to her to go have fun but all she did was work, work, work, with running as her only outlet to relax and let off steam. As he had gotten to know Finn this past year, he became convinced that he was exactly the kind of man that Bella would like. So, he bided

his time until he was sure, deliberately not giving them any information about the other, until he set the stage for tonight.

So far so good, it seems, he thought. *I'll give them five more minutes and then I'll join them.*

When Hank finally descended the stairs and hugged Finn warmly, Bella looked at the clock in confusion. It had just occurred to her that Finn had been in the house for thirty minutes now and yet Hank had only just come downstairs this second. She looked over at Hank with an accusing expression on her face. She knew a set up when she saw one and this was a big one. Hank shrugged innocently at her then turned away to get out of the line of fire.

Dinner was fun. Bella had put together a wonderful spread and Finn had to plead for mercy as she produced dish after dish.

"I won't be able to walk tomorrow not to mind run," he groaned when he finally pushed back from the table.

"Oh, you run, do you?" Bella asked with surprise in her voice. "Really, I wouldn't have guessed."

Hank smiled to himself. He had been right. He could tell from the comments back and forth all evening that they were quite intrigued with each other.

"Oh, I don't go far. Probably nothing on the scale you do. You do run, don't you?"

Before Bella could respond, Hank interjected, "Maybe you guys could quit talking about running and actually go for a run together sometime. Seems to me that would be the only way to resolve this little impasse we have going on here."

Both Bella and Finn dismissed that suggestion out of hand with Bella giving one reason and Finn another, but Hank could see they were thinking about it. They were falling nicely into the trap he was setting for them and he was having such fun doing it.

After dinner was over, they washed up and Hank suggested they go sit outside. It was still warm and pleasant even though it was well after ten. Hank broke out his special occasion bourbon and poured each of them a stiff shot. Then he downed his and stood up quickly.

"Well, that's it for me. These old bones need their rest. Some of us have to work in the morning. I'm going to leave this bottle right here so you young folks go right ahead and help yourselves."

He turned to Finn and stuck out his hand.

"Goodnight, my friend. It was great seeing you as always. I'm sorry it took so long for me to get you here but you must definitely come back again. Isn't that right, Bella?"

Hank could feel the daggers from Bella without even turning around. He knew by now that she had seen through his ploy and would not be impressed at being set up. His only hope to escape her wrath was that she had found Finn sufficiently interesting that she might go easy on her conniving grandfather.

"Most certainly, Grandfather," he heard her say.

Nope, he thought, *I'm not out of the woods yet.*

He had learned a long time ago that when Bella called him 'grandfather', she was angry about something with him. It had been a long, long time since she had called him that but here she was, doing it tonight.

Hank bent to kiss on top of her head and said, "Goodnight, sweetheart. Thanks for cooking such a wonderful meal. I truly enjoyed it."

As headed inside, he heard her response, "Goodnight, Grandfather."

Well, I'll be damned, he thought. *Twice in one night. Better lay low tomorrow.*

Finn had watched the little exchange with amusement. He too had realized that Hank had set them up and he knew that for all Bella's efforts to act annoyed, she wasn't the least bit. They sat in silence for a few minutes sipping their drinks. Each of them was running appraisals of the other in their minds and so far, they were giving high marks. Bella turned to Finn.

"Would you like to go for a walk? It's nice down by the river and it's not that far."

Fin looked back at her, studying her face to see if the last part of the sentence was intended as a challenge. Once again, Bella's beautiful face was a picture of absolute innocence. Finn drained his glass, stood up, and replied, "Yes, I'd love to. I suppose I could always try to carry you if you can't make it back."

Then he jumped off the porch before Bella could reach him and punch him.

Chapter Twenty-Four
April 1989
Edgarville, Kentucky

Finn sat in his apartment thinking. It was well after three in the morning but he had just gotten home. He and Bella had walked for miles, talking the whole time. He had opened up completely to her and told her his whole story and he gave all the details of Julia and Siodhraidh and how their deaths still haunted him each and every day.

At some point during the walk as Finn spoke, Bella had slipped her hand into his. It had felt so natural that Finn didn't react as he would have had under any other circumstance with any other person. Every now and then when she seemed to sense that he was struggling with his emotions or when she thought he was at a very difficult part of the story, Bella would rub her thumb against his and squeeze his hand a little tighter. It was her way of encouraging him to keep going while letting him know that she understood how difficult it was for him.

He was very touched by this gesture and very appreciative. Although he had only just met her that

evening, Finn knew there was something special about Bella. Something really trustworthy.

As he sat there recalling the evening, Finn smiled at how easy the banter between them had been and how it had been replaced by kind comments when the discussion became serious. He had felt like he could have kept walking all night but eventually they had found their way back to the street where Bella lived.

"So," she said as they stood on the porch, "will you get up early to go running?"

"I hope so but it is way past my bedtime so we'll have to see."

"If you do, I'd like to tag along."

Finn looked at her standing there as he pieced his response together in his mind first. He always ran alone and much as he had enjoyed Bella's company tonight, running together wouldn't work. Before he had processed his thought completely, he heard Bella say, "You know I've noticed that when you're about to say no to something and you're thinking about how best to put it, you scrunch up your face. It's like you're trying so hard to get your brain working that you use your face muscles as well to help get it moving faster. I noticed this a few times earlier as well and you just did it again there. So, I'm assuming that it's a 'no'. Am I right?"

Finn laughed then looked at her seriously.

"I'm sorry. It's just that I have this routine that I like to stick to. It's got nothing to do with you. It's just how I am about certain things."

"I understand. Well, sort of anyways. I mean it must be a hell of a routine if you can't break it just once to go for a

run with a girl who's standing here asking you to do so. Alright then, how about dinner?"

Before Finn could even open his mouth, Bella exclaimed, "Jesus, you just did it again. You scrunched up your fucking face as soon as I mentioned dinner. I tell you what, Finn Lane, you have such a way of making a girl feel good about herself. No way could she begin to have any doubts watching you contort your ugly mug six ways to Sunday."

Finn initially thought she was upset with him but then he noticed that her eyes were smiling and that she was teasing him.

"Not funny," he protested. "I…"

He stopped talking after Bella gently took his face in her hands.

"I what?" she said tenderly. "I know what you've been through and I'm not coming on to you. I like your company and it seems to me that both of us could do with another friend in our lives. I'm not trying to make you uncomfortable or put you in awkward situation. Honest. I understand."

To his own total surprise, Finn then said, "Dinner it is. Pick a night next week. Any night. I have no conflicts or other plans."

Bella laughed and let go of his face.

"See what I mean about us needing other people in our lives. I'm open every night myself with no conflicts or plans. Wednesday so? I'll let you choose the venue and the time."

"Deal. I'll come by at seven. I don't have a car so we can walk or grab a taxi."

"That's alright," Bella responded. "I have a car. I'll come get you instead. Thanks for a very nice night, Finn."

She hugged him briefly and went in.

Now sitting here in his apartment, he worried if he had done the right thing. He felt guilty about taking Bella out to dinner though he was certain that Julia would completely understand and would want him to do this. It didn't feel quite right but he had committed to it so he would follow through. He was also, he admitted, looking forward to it. Bella had been a wonderful pick me up tonic for him this evening and he did want to see her again.

Chapter Twenty-Five
April 1989
Edgarville, Kentucky

Finn hadn't gone running the next morning. He had sat in his apartment so long that it was almost starting to get bright when he went to bed and it had been noon before he woke up. He went to his office to catch up on some work for the afternoon and then headed to the gym for a workout. He was back in training for an MMA cage fighting tournament that was going to take place in Las Vegas next month.

This tournament had attracted the best fighters from around the country as well as internationally. It would be a tough, no-holds barred, competition where only the toughest would survive. There were barely any rules in cage fighting so it was no place for the faint of heart. Finn was looking forward to it. He had always fought hard but after Julia's and Siodhraidh's deaths, he also fought angry now. This was a lethal combination and one his opponents would suffer as a result of.

The next morning after he finished his run, he sat with Hank in the warm sunshine.

"You sly old dog," he said with a mixture of irritation and admiration in his voice, "you played both of us. I'm betting your granddaughter gave you an earful. She looks like she could be fiery when she gets mad."

Hank looked over at him, a grin a mile long plastered on his face.

"First, how about thank you, Hank, for not being mad that you kept my granddaughter out until almost three. Second, you have no idea the amount of grief I got from her. Went off on me like a banshee. My poor ears are still ringing. And you what the best part is; the girl didn't mean one word of it. She's as happy as a clam and looking forward to going to dinner with you."

Putting on his best woe is me act, Hank continued, "And not a lick of thanks from either of you. Just goes to show. Young people today. No gratitude."

Finn let him rattle on. He was grateful to Hank and he was pleased in a way to hear that Bella was looking forward to going out to dinner with him. Then he heard Hank say.

"Now listen to me, Finn, this is important. We're in the South and it's still frowned upon in certain quarters for a white man to take a black woman out. You can't just think that you can go into any restaurant in town and expect them to put the welcome mat out for you. It doesn't work like that.

"Also, you need to be prepared for comments and nasty looks to come your way. I know it's 1989 but old thinking dies very slowly down here. So be careful. I don't want Bella to be put in any bad situation."

Finn stared at Hank. He knew that everything his friend had said was true and he would never expose Bella to any

danger but he'd be goddamned if he'd look the other way if they got any abuse.

"I know," he replied. "I'll be careful but I want you to know, I will never let anyone say or do anything to hurt Bella when she's in my company. Never."

Hank looked at him. He had heard the vehemence in Finn's voice. He also knew what Finn was capable of.

"I know that, son. I know that."

Chapter Twenty-Six
April 1989
Edgarville, Kentucky

Finn was standing outside when Bella drove up in her car. He had decided to dress up for the occasion and he had put on a well-fitting black suit, dark blue shirt and a blue and yellow tie. Bella was so distracted by the handsome figure he cut that she nearly mounted the sidewalk as she pulled up. She got out with a grin on her face.

"Aren't I supposed to knock at the door or something? Isn't that what the person with the car does?"

"Stop," Finn replied. "I'm self-conscious enough already about the fact that you had to come get me and I don't need you rubbing it in."

"Don't be silly," she laughed. "Besides, you're paying for dinner, right?"

Finn deliberately scrunched up his face and stared blankly at Bella.

"Hah, nice try bucko, but no dice. I'm not falling for that. By the way, you look very handsome tonight."

"Shouldn't I be the one complimenting you?" he asked.

"You should but since I wasn't hearing any compliments coming my way, I figured one of us at least should have some manners."

"Well," Finn said, "for what it's worth and late or not, I can tell you, Bella, you look stunning."

He wasn't exaggerating. She did. She wore tan, tight-fitting pants, a baby blue shirt and three-inch heels. With her hair pulled up, she looked absolutely regal.

"Come on now, enough of this chit-chatting. This girl is hungry," Bella replied deflecting his compliment. Finn could tell that she was pleased though and he was happy for that. When they were in the car, Bella asked where they were going. When Finn gave her the name of the restaurant, a strange look came across her face. Finn caught it immediately.

"What's the matter? Isn't it any good? It came highly recommended by several people."

"No, it's not that," Bella replied. "I'm sure the food is great. I don't know. I've never been there."

"Then what's the problem?" Finn asked not putting two and two together.

"Look, to be blunt. It's not the kind of establishment that exactly welcomes people like me or would be comfortable with a mixed race as couple as guests. There it is. Now you know."

"Christ, I'm sorry, Bella," Finn said despondently, "I should have checked that more carefully. I kind of thought that since it's an upmarket establishment that this would not be an issue."

"You would think, right?" said Bella bitterly. "But the more upmarket the establishment the lighter skin color of the acceptable clientele. Fact of life, Finn dear. Fact of life."

"Look Bella, no problem. We can go somewhere else. Honest. Hey, you can even come in and we'll order pizza."

She laughed at that. Her good humor returning but she shook her head defiantly.

"No. Let's go. To hell with them. If they don't like it, they can lump it."

"My kind of girl," Finn exclaimed. "Let's do it."

They chatted easily on the way to the restaurant though Finn had a nagging thought in the back of his mind that maybe it would be better to go somewhere else. It was a busy spot and they could only find parking about a block away. Finn was conscious of several stares at them as they walked back to the restaurant but he wasn't sure if they were nasty looks or just plain admiration of Bella.

The maître-d looked at them frostily as they entered and was quick to say, "We're very full tonight. We're not taking walk-ins, I'm afraid."

Finn was not exactly overjoyed by his tone but he kept his own light as he responded, "That's no problem. We have a reservation. Lane. Table for two at seven-thirty."

He glanced around the restaurant. There were only a few tables occupied right now but he thought it was possible that the others could fill up any time. He looked back at the maître-d who was shaking his head as he looked at the reservation list.

"No, I'm sorry. There must be a misunderstanding. I don't see your name here at all, I'm afraid."

This guy was seriously beginning to piss Finn off. He knew he had a reservation and, in fact, the restaurant itself had called today to confirm it, as was their policy. Frustrated, he reached over suddenly, pulled the book from the guy's hands, and said, "I think you must have missed it. There it is. Lane. Table for two. Seven-thirty, Wednesday. So, guess what? It's Wednesday, it's seven-thirty and we're here. So can you show us to our table, please?"

There was just enough edge in his voice to make the other man nervous. He clearly wasn't happy but he had no choice now but to seat them. Finn glanced at Bella but she didn't seem like she was upset.

Maybe she's just conditioned to it, he thought but he certainly wasn't.

After they were seated at their table, things went further downhill. Service was appallingly slow, the waiter's attitude was disgraceful, and their food was either overcooked or half-raw. As the evening wore on, Finn got angrier and angrier. It was hard to keep the conversation going under these circumstances and it faltered several times.

Bella seemed to withdraw inside herself and she clearly wasn't having a good time. This annoyed Finn even more; he had wanted her to enjoy herself. Every now and then he'd catch a snigger or a sneer from a nearby table which only served to add to his frustration. Finally, mercifully, the meal was over. If the waiters were slow in getting them their food, they were lightning fast in getting the check to them. Finn paid and did not leave a tip.

He longed to say something to the snooty maître-d, to the horrible staff and those disproving other guests but he held his tongue for Bella's sake. Barely, but he did.

When they stepped outside, they were both frustrated and angry. They had each being looking forward to spending time together but it had been spoiled by a bunch of bigots. Then Bella said, "I forgot my cardigan. I left it on the chair."

"I'll get it," Finn told her. "No reason for you to go back in there again. Will you wait here?"

"If you don't mind, I'd like to get as far away as possible from here so I'll walk to the car and wait for you there."

"Are you sure? I'll just be a minute."

"Yes, I'm sure. I'll meet you at the car."

Finn walked back in to the restaurant. He was pleased to note that the place went quiet when he pushed through the door. He stared at the maître-d with a look of total disgust that made the man wince. Without saying a word to anyone, he walked slowly and deliberately to the table where they had sat. Bella's cardigan was still on the chair. He picked it up, swept the room deliberately with his eyes then headed back to the door. Along the way, he stopped at the maître-d's desk, stared into his face, and in a very low voice he said, "You are a disgusting little prick. I just thought you should know that."

He felt a little better as he walked to the car. When he got there, there was no sign of Bella. Puzzled, he looked around. He then heard a muffled scream from an alleyway down a nearby side street and ran towards it as fast as he could. He knew something had happened to Bella. When he

got to the front of the alleyway, he could see Bella about halfway down, surrounded by three men.

They were clearly harassing her. He began to run towards them and as he got closer, he saw one of the men raise his hand to strike Bella, Finn snapped. Everything that had been building up in him all night came out in a torrent. He caught the man's arm just above his wrist in mid-air and stopped it cold.

He then squeezed the man's hand with all his strength until he could hear the bones break in his arm. In a fluid movement, he pivoted and kneed the guy full force in the groin before slamming his elbow into his ear as hard as he could. As the first guy fell to the ground, Finn rounded on a second one and head butted him viciously in the bridge of his nose, which cracked instantly. He then swept the guy's legs from under him and when he was on the ground, Finn stomped him hard twice on the nose that he had just broken.

All the while, Bella had been screaming at him to stop but Finn couldn't he was too angry. The third guy, having seen what had happened his friends, started to run down the alley.

"Oh no you don't," Finn shouted as he ran after him.

"Let him go, Finn, please," Bella pleaded. "That's enough. You've already done too much damage."

But even that couldn't stop him. He was in a total rage by now. He caught the guy easily and punched him savagely several times until he felt Bella pulling at him and begging him to stop. He left the guy drop to the ground.

"What have you done?" she screamed angry at him now. "You didn't need to nearly kill them. Look at them. You went too far."

She was spitting fire now and it was all directed at Finn.

"I'm sorry, Bella. They were going to hurt you. I couldn't let that happen. I promised Hank I'd take care of you."

"Take care of me, take care of me," she spat at him. "You call this taking care of me. For fuck's sake, Finn. You could have just stopped them. You didn't need to do this."

"I'm sorry," he replied not entirely sure why she was so angry at him. "I guess I lost it. With all that had been building up tonight, I just couldn't let it go anymore."

But Bella was not to be placated. She was disgusted by the brutality he had displayed.

"You're so fucking selfish, Finn," she said bitterly. "You had to endure a bit of hassle for a few hours and you couldn't take it. I've been living with that shit all my fucking life. This is my life. Grow the fuck up, okay."

Finn was stunned. Her anger was total. She looked like she could punch him any second. He stuttered, "I'm sorry, Julia, I…"

The words were out of his mouth before he could catch them and he instantly regretted them.

"Julia, Julia? I'm not Julia. I'm fucking Bella. You know the girl you were supposed to be with tonight. You know what you're fucking problem is Finn Lane. You live in the past. I'm sorry to say it but Julia is gone. She's not coming back. Go ahead and live your fucking miserable little life in the past, you shithead.

"I don't need you dragging me back there with you and ending up as fucking miserable as you. Go on. Go ahead. Be miserable as you feel completely sorry for yourself but

you're not going to do that to me. So fuck off. I'm going home. You can find you own way home, asshole."

She strode towards the car and drove away quickly. Finn stood there and stared at the three guys who were still lying on the floor and who had witnessed Bella's tirade. Then he walked out of the alley.

He had blown it completely. He was still rather taken aback by Bella's reaction. It's possible that he had overdone it but he was just looking out for her. On the other hand, maybe it was for the best. He didn't need the complication that Bella would surely bring to his life.

Chapter Twenty-Seven
April 1989
Edgarville, Kentucky

Finn couldn't tell the next morning if Hank was aware how his night out with Bella had ended. He hadn't acted any differently with Finn and his face was totally inscrutable. Finally, Finn couldn't bear it anymore.

"Did Bella say anything to you about last night?" he asked finally, trying to keep his voice as casually sounding as possible.

"Nope. Should she?" was all Hank said.

"No. I don't know. I guess not."

Hank looked at him inquisitively.

"That's a lot of movement of position in one sentence, my friend. Is there something you want to tell me? Because my granddaughter sure as hell won't."

"No," Finn replied. "Not at all."

Throughout the test of the day and on into the weekend, Finn kept replaying the night over and over in his mind. He knew he had over reacted but still some of the things that Bella had said puzzled him. He had learned one thing for

certain from the whole experience, Bella had one hell of a temper when she got going and a mouth to match it.

He debated constantly whether to call her or go see her but each time he ended up deciding against it. What could he possibly say to make things right? And, in any event, she hadn't exactly left even the tiniest crack in the door open that could lead him to believe that she might even be remotely interested in speaking to him again. He had to let it go. It wasn't like he had known her long or well anyway. It had only been two nights.

When Hank invited him over for dinner that Friday evening, Finn's first thought was that Bella was behind it. After all, he reasoned, she wouldn't want him coming over to her house if she wasn't willing to be friends again. He found himself growing happier and happier at the thought of seeing her again and welcomed the opportunity to make things right.

That evening he dressed carefully, making sure he looked his best. He had bought flowers and wine that afternoon as well as some beer for Hank. He wondered what concoction she would prepare tonight. Dinner at her house the last time had been excellent so he was really looking forward to her next creation. He was glad this was happening. They could draw a line in the sand, put the unhappy events of the past week behind them and move on.

Finn rang the doorbell and waited. He smiled at the memory of how surprised they had both been that first time they met. He was ready this time. Instead, though, it was Hank who opened the door. He looked puzzled when he saw the flowers and the wine.

"Those for me? You shouldn't have."

"Yes. The wine and the flowers are for you and the beer is for your granddaughter," Finn replied happily, pleased at his quick wit. But Hank just shook his head.

"Well, I guess I get the beer also because Bella ain't here. Didn't she tell you that? She told me you knew that she wouldn't be here tonight when you were coming over."

Finn was deflated. He had not for one minute countenanced the possibility that Bella wouldn't be home. She was clearly sending him a message. He felt totally foolish now standing there with the wine and flowers.

"I guess we got our lines crossed. I think I misunderstood the situation."

"Not to worry," Hank said encouragingly. "Come on in and we'll open a beer and eat some pizza."

There goes the gourmet dinner as well, Finn thought bitterly.

He still had a good time though. Hank was good company and he had an amazing repertoire of stories of his early years, the war and, of course, horses. Throughout the evening, Finn kept wondering if Bella would show up but even though it was after eleven when he finally left, there was no sign of her.

He walked him slowly. He had completely misread the situation. Bella was not looking to mend fences with him. She had meant what she said. She didn't want him in her life in any way, shape or form. Much and all as he tried to convince himself that it was for the best, that he didn't need the complication, he knew deep down that he really liked her.

Such a shame, he thought as he kicked idly at a stone. *It could have been good.*

For the next couple of weeks, his life settled back into its regular pattern. Bella had been a brief interlude, a moment of respite, but nothing else. Reality intervened. So, he worked, he trained and he had dinner with Hank, each time at Finn's apartment though.

Finally, the weekend of the tournament in Las Vegas came around. He had told Hank about it and asked him to come along but Hank had declined telling Finn that he was too old to travel that far. Finn was glad in a way that Bella wasn't in his life right now. He doubted that she'd be too impressed with the whole concept of cage fighting.

Finn had gotten himself in great physical shape and he was at the peak of his power as a fighter. If he had any concerns, it was over the anger that bubbled just below the surface. It worried him that he might actually end up being too aggressive and seriously hurt someone. He knew, of course, that his opponents were all highly trained, skillful fighters and not some thugs on a street but even so, this anger that he felt made him concerned.

It turned out that he was right to be concerned. After he had completed his first two fights and saw the state his opponents had been left in, he knew he had to withdraw from the competition. He was convinced, it wasn't fair for him to continue. Besides, he was sure that he caught sight of Bella a couple of times in the crowd. She had been wearing a hat and sunglasses to mask her identity but he felt certain it was her. So, he pulled out and headed home. He would fight again but not for a while until the rage inside him had fully receded.

The month of May rolled into June and the end of classes start loom. Soon, all the students would head home

for the summer and the college would enter a zone of tranquility. Finn really liked the interaction he had with his students but those summer months were a welcome and refreshing relief. He planned to go to Ireland in July for a week. It was time to go visit Julia and Siodhraidh's graves. July would be nice there where they were buried. He could sit and look at the mountains and the sea and be at peace in his thoughts with them. He needed to spend time with them now. It was making him edgy; it had been so long.

Finn looked at the clock on his office wall. It was after seven. Through his open window, he could tell that it was a very pleasant evening. He decided to call it quits for the day and maybe take a long walk. With the bright evenings and the warm air, this was a perfect time of year to go walking.

As he exited the department building, he stopped dead in his tracks. There, sitting on a bench was Bella. He was amazed. It had been almost two months since had last seen her and he really believed they would never see each other again. It was clear she was waiting for him but he wondered why. He strolled over to the bench taking her in with his eyes.

Still gorgeous, he thought. *Definitely a sight for sore eyes.*

He reached the bench and stopped. He figured that since she had come to see him, she had something to say.

"Hi Finn. Long time no see. Got a few minutes to sit and chat?"

"It has been a long time. It's nice to see you. I got nowhere special to be."

"Aha," Bella said with a grin. "Still living a life free of complications."

She stopped herself.

"I'm sorry. That didn't come out right. I'm not here to insult you. I've brought a peace offering."

Finn looked at her.

"What's that?"

Bella put a straight face on.

"A peace offering is when one person brings something to another person to show them they're sorry and that they want to be friends."

Finn scrunched up his face deliberately and stared silently at her. Bella reached out and took his face in her hands and attempted to un-scrunch it.

"Not the scrunched-up face, please. I can take anything but that harbinger of bad news, disappointment, and impending heartache."

Finn laughed, enjoying the pressure of her hands on his face.

"Actually, while I do thank you for the dictionary lesson, I really meant what did you bring as a peace offering?"

"You're welcome," Bella responded. "Happy to demonstrate my erudition anytime. As for the peace offering. Well, let me see. How does a glass of my grandfather's favorite bourbon grab you?"

She reached into her bag and pulled out a bottle and two glasses.

"What, you mean here? I like the idea but I'm not convinced the college would be happy to see a staff member sitting on a bench drinking."

"No," Bella replied, "I was kind of hoping we could take a walk down to the river. There's a couple of nice

picnic spots there where we could sit and drink and talk. I have quite a bit of explaining to do and quite a bit of apologizing to do."

"Sounds good to me," Finn grinned. "I certainly agree."

"Shut up. Don't push your luck. We're not on solid enough ground for that yet."

Bella's eyes were smiling as she spoke the last sentence.

"Seems to me," said Finn solemnly, "there's a strong foundation being put in right now."

He jumped up and down.

"Yessiree. I do believe that's the case."

He stood and waited for Bella to get up. When she did, she pressed herself against and kissed him slowly and tenderly full on his lips. Her voice was husky as she said, "You have no idea how badly I wanted to do that. No idea at all."

Finn had kissed her back. His head was swimming wildly. This had been such an unexpected turn of events. When they had finished, Bella took his hand and they began to walk towards the river. He could already feel some of that rage beginning to recede.

Chapter Twenty-Eight
June 1989
Edgarville, Kentucky

They strolled slowly towards the river. Neither of them spoke much but it seemed fine to Finn. There were no awkward silences. Instead, he felt a sort of peaceable companionship in the air. Every now and then Bella would rub his thumb with hers as she held his hand, exerting just enough pressure to send a warm sensation coursing through his arm and out into his body. He liked the way she did it. Randomly and briefly.

When they reached the river, they sat a picnic bench and Bella poured them each a shot of bourbon. She raised her glass.

"To understanding that they don't put signs out there telling you that you're at the end of the rainbow. Put another way, to not making comparisons and judgements when there's really no need."

Finn looked at her. He understood what she meant. They had both known instantly that there could be something special between them but that in their anxiety to not let their respective baggage get in the way, they had set their sights

on perfection. Since that didn't exist in real life, disappointment, anger, and hurt had virtually ruined their relationship before it had properly started.

"I'll drink to that," Finn replied, looking her in the eye and clinking his glass against hers. Bella took a deep slug.

"Okay," she said. "Now, I'm going to talk for a while, it could be a long while and you're going to listen and let me speak. Deal?"

Finn nodded his head. "Deal."

"Excellent."

She took another drink.

"One more thing first, though."

Then she leaned over and kissed him again. This was a very different kiss to the earlier one. Now Finn could sense the passion, the need on her lips and her tongue as it probed his mouth. He could taste the sweetness of the bourbon she had just drunk on her breath and it heightened the experience. He kissed her back with equal fervor, equal passion.

"Wow," Bella exclaimed when the kiss ended. She began to fan herself with a magazine she pulled from her bag.

"My, my. I'm just glad I'm sitting down right now. I honestly don't think my legs could carry me anywhere. You're going to have to give me a moment to collect my thoughts. My brain is a tad scrambled at the present."

Finn smiled. He knew what she meant. He had also been whisked away to some magical place during that kiss and it was proving difficult to recalibrate his heart, his mind and even his breathing.

All that from just one kiss, he thought to himself. *Makes you wonder.*

"Okay, finally," Bella declared. "Now, I'm ready."

She took one more drink from her glass and started to speak.

"First, a confession. I went to Las Vegas to see you fight. I figured you saw me but I just wanted to confirm that I was actually there. It was funny the way it happened actually. My grandfather, who I never said anything to about what happened between us, mentioned casually that you were heading to Vegas to compete in a fighting tournament and, in that split second, I said I knew and that I was going with you.

"He seemed so happy about it that I felt really bad deceiving him. I knew he wondered why you hadn't come around much or why I was never home the couple of times you did but he's not the kind of man to pry so just kept his own counsel. Anyway, I went and watched you. It was terrifying, I'll be honest, to see the ferocity you fought with and I was so glad that you pulled out.

"I admired you completely for that, you know. Everyone else was totally pissed off when the announcement was made but I understood. That was a very brave thing to do. And you know, even though I hated to watch you fight, it ended up being completely therapeutic for me."

She paused and took a breath. Smiled at him and continued.

"So now, we've hit the apology part of my soliloquy. I judged you, Finn. Plain and simple. I put you in a box and made a decision about you and that was wrong. You see,

and this is not me justifying anything, it's just an explanation, I come from a line of women for whom falling in love is practically fatal. Literally, fatal.

"My grandmother defied the conventions of her status in life and centuries old traditions to run away with a poor, black farmhand then died in childbirth. I know that could have happened anyway but I truly believe it was a result of all the stress and strain on her and their relationship. My mother; well, we've no idea who my mother fell for actually but I think we can safely assume that it wasn't the nice boy next door.

"Then she was murdered for her beliefs when I was just a baby. I have no memory of her and I'll never, ever know who my father is. So, to me, my life has always been shaped by violence and pain and suffering. That's why I never wanted to get involved with anyone or let anyone get close to me. I was afraid there was some kind of curse in our family and someone, most likely me, would end up badly hurt or dead."

She stopped again. Looked at him appraisingly, trying to read any signals in his face or eyes. But Finn just held gaze steadily. This was not a time for jokes or wise cracks and he knew it. Whatever, happened here during and after Bella's story had the potential to alter the course of his life forever. So, Finn just nodded his head in encouragement.

"Good, okay. I was beginning to think that I was rambling all over the place. Anyway, as I was saying. I never wanted to let anyone get close to me so no one did. Then you came along and in an instant, you shattered every single one of my resolutions. Poof, just like that they were gone. I've always scoffed at the idea of love at first sight. In

my analytical mind, I always believed that it couldn't be possible that love had to grow from an understanding of the other person and couldn't just happen in the blink of an eye."

Bella stood up suddenly and walked towards the river. Finn watched her go but didn't say anything. There was already a lot to process and he had the sense that whatever she was going to say next was critically important to her and most likely to him.

At the edge of the river, Bella bent down and picked up some stones that she sent skimming across the surface of the water. Finn, counting the number of hops each made on the surface before sinking, was very impressed. She was very skillful. He could tell that she seemed to be having some kind of an internal debate. After a few minutes, she stood and nodded her head emphatically as if she had at last reached a decision. She walked purposefully back to the bench, head down, chewing on a strand of her hair.

"Sorry about that, Finn," she said as she sat down, "I needed a moment."

"No problem, this is tough sledding. For what it's worth, I think you're doing great. You're being very brave."

Bella laughed at that.

"Yeah well, that's one thing about the women in our family. We might not make the smartest of decisions but there's no shortage of courage."

She looked directly at Finn.

"Anyway, I was saying that I didn't believe that love at first sight was possible. Well, you know what? I was totally wrong. Now don't go getting a big head and all that on me now, but when I opened that door and saw you standing

there for the very first time, I fell instantly and totally head over heels in love you. It was amazing. It was like this invisible force just leaped from your body into mine and captured me. Literally, I felt a physical reaction as much as an emotional one. I was yours from that moment on, plain and simple."

She paused again. This time she looked at him quite sheepishly as she continued to search for clues in his expression. She knew she had put it all out there now and there was no taking back those words, they would always exist either as a barrier or a bond between them. Finn continued to hold her gaze evenly and steadily, giving nothing away about how he might be reacting to her words or what he was thinking.

Bella continued on, "I can't actually believe I just right out and said all that but there you go. You know, in my mind it sounded way more eloquent and romantic than it did right there out loud. But, oh well, I'm pretty sure you got the drift. Anyway, I know you're thinking that this is supposed to be an apology and it is and I will get there. I'm just giving you deep background first. I guess it's the lawyer in me.

"I feel like I'm making my case before a jury. I want to build it painstakingly so that you'll find me, well not innocent because I admit I was wrong, but that you'll find me forgivable. So yeah, I fell madly in love with you and after that first night and before we went for dinner, I created these scenarios in my head: we were going to be the perfect couple, white picket fence, wonderful kids, great neighbors, the whole nine yards of *It's a Wonderful Life*.

"I didn't just jump ahead. I went to the moon and back. I planned a whole future out in my mind for us and in my

mind it was perfect. And then this gritty, ugly world we live in dragged me headlong back to reality and, to top it all, the violence that I feared that dogged my family's history was happening again right before my eyes. I lost it. Completely and totally. I'm so sorry. I said so many hurtful things to you. Especially when you called me Julia."

She reached out and touched his face gently.

"That was so monstrous of me. I am so ashamed of those words. And the language I used. I think I packed more bad language into those few minutes than I had in my whole life before then. So, you see, or at least I hope you do, I created an artificial future scenario in my mind to insulate myself from the realities of my past and my present and when the inevitable happened, I couldn't cope. So, I just judged you as another violent pig that I didn't want or need in my life."

Bella poured them both another drink. She had been talking a long time by now. The sun had gone completely down and stars were starting to dot the sky. She had tears in her eyes when she continued, "I hated myself so intensely after that night. I literally was disgusted by myself. It's like I'd look in the mirror and see this despicable creature staring back at me. I kept saying to myself 'this isn't me, this isn't me' but in the back of my head I wondered if it actually wasn't me and if I really am a horrible person underneath it all."

Bella waited to see if Finn was going to jump in and say anything but he remained implacable as he sat there.

"So, when my grandfather said about Vegas, it was almost like a sign to me. The worst thing for me about you was the violence you displayed so I figured going to Vegas,

right there to a location, where that violence would be on display would either kill me or cure me. And it cured me. It made me understand you and who you and what you are.

"And most importantly, it made me understand that I was still truly madly in love with you and not having you in my life would be such a waste, a useless meaningless waste. So, I struggled for ages to pluck up the courage until tonight I was ready."

She reached out to him, touched his face, then ran her fingers through his hair.

'Listen to me now, Finn, this important. I don't know how you feel about me and I don't want you to tell me. I don't care if it's good or bad, don't say it. At least not yet. And I don't want to replace Julia or Siodhraidh in your life or in your heart. I'll take whatever slice you're willing to give me. It will be more than enough.

"So, that's what I meant about there being no signs saying you're at the end of the rainbow and there's the crock of gold waiting for you. I'm already there. I know that now. So, all I want for now is to spend time with you, get to know you better, maybe go for a run with you sometime, whatever. If it builds from there, great. If not, great. I'll be spending time with the person I love. What's not to want about that?"

She raised her glass.

"Finally, after all that. Please forgive me and be my friend."

Finn lifted his glass and touched it against Bella's and looked deeply into her eyes. He knew how difficult it was for her to say what she had. This had been raw, unfiltered emotion, free of agenda or motive. It was simply Bella

opening her heart for him to see, for him to decide where or if she would fit in his life. He admired her courage and her willingness to take such a huge risk.

Finn drained his glass, stood up walked around the bench to Bella's side and sat down next to her. Then he pulled her into his arms until she was sitting on his lap and kissed her with a force that took her breath away. When it was finished, Finn looked at her, smiled and said, "Friends."

He could see the lump in her throat and the tears in her eyes as she struggled with her emotions but she still managed to say.

"That's it? One word? I give you a speech as long as *War and Peace* and you give me a single word in return."

"Yep. One word. Anything more would be redundant."

They stood up and Finn said, "Let's get you home."

When they got there, Finn turned Bella towards him.

"Look Bella, I want to spend time with you too. I was lost without you. I kept telling myself it was for the best but I didn't believe it. But you have to be patient with me. I don't have your whole unbroken heart. Mine has been shattered into many pieces, there are parts of it that are completely closed off from this world. I don't even know how to reach them anymore. I know there's a place for you but I don't know how much that is or even how to get there. I need to go slowly here and it may end up hurting and frustrating you."

Bella shook her head.

"What you just said there is more than I even allowed myself to hope for. I'll find whatever cracks there are that will let me in. I'm in no hurry. I got the rest of my life."

She hugged him, wished him goodnight and went in. When she closed the door behind her, Bella leaned her back against the wall then slowly slid down until she was sitting on the floor. She began to cry, great heaving sobs. Upstairs in his bedroom, Hank heard her and he smiled. He had been around long enough to recognize tears of joy when he heard them.

Finn walked home slowly. He found himself more at peace than he had been for the longest time.

Chapter Twenty-Nine
July 1989
Edgarville, Kentucky

Finn wasn't exactly sure any longer if it had been two, three, or even four weeks since that night at the river with Bella, the time seemed to have gone by so rapidly. They saw each other three or four times a week now and their relationship deepened after each date. Anxious to avoid a repeat of the fiasco at the restaurant, Finn deliberately stayed away from venues that could prove to be a potential flashpoint.

He was well aware that this strategy of avoidance could only continue for so long but he believed that right now, at this juncture in their relationship, discretion was definitely the better point of valor. So, they went on lots of long walks or drove to secluded spots where they could be alone and talk freely.

They had not kissed again since that night. Bella was determined to go at Finn's pace so she backed off and waited for him to make the first move. This was proving to be an amazingly difficult challenge. Every fiber of her body ached for him. She yearned to feel his arms around her, his lips on hers, his hands touching her, and she wanted to feel

him inside her. She had no sexual experience whatsoever. She had never felt real physical attraction to any man before but now her very skin crawled with desire.

It was also proving harder and harder to say goodnight to Finn and watch him walk away. She wanted to be with him all the time and would have loved to snuggle next to him in bed, whether they actually made love or not.

For Finn, on the other hand, things were moving at a very rapid pace, too rapid at times. He was starting to fall heavily for Bella but his heart and mind were not yet ready to make the leap into a full and committed relationship. He wondered if they weren't actually seeing too much of each other too soon. The road back from the desolate place he had found himself after murder of his wife and daughter was incredibly rocky and there were no clear directions to follow.

He was determined to return to feeling normal but he still woke up at night with an aching void in his heart. There were times when he could almost hear baby Siodhraidh gurgling contentedly or feel her lying in his arms or even at times he thought he caught a whiff of the scent of her fresh baby smell after she had just been bathed.

Other times, he could hear Julia's voice as she sang to Siodhraidh or when she cried out as they made love. It was all so very confusing and he was constantly conflicted. His physical desire for Bella grew stronger every day but he was just not ready to take that step. He could sense how difficult it was all becoming for Bella and while he truly appreciated her patience, he knew it wasn't going to be infinite.

In a sense then, he was almost relieved that his trip to Ireland was looming closer. It would give them both some

breathing room and maybe allow the simmering tension that he was increasingly sensing some time to cool off.

They were out for yet another walk when Finn said to Bella, "It won't be long now to my trip back to Ireland. Just over a week, actually."

Bella said nothing at first but Finn noticed that she had rubbed his thumb with hers a couple of times during the silence. Like a poker player, this was one of Bella's 'tells'. It invariably meant there was something going on in her mind and she was marshaling her thoughts to get the words straight. He waited.

"Can I come with you?"

There it was. She had said it. Bella had been working up to this for over a week now and each time she got close to saying it, she had chickened out. Then out of the blue, Finn had given her an opening and she knew it was now or never. She turned to look at him to gauge his reaction.

"No, no, no. Don't you do that. Do not scrunch your face. Not now."

Finn smiled back at her. "I won't, I promise."

Before he could say anything else she butted in, "I know it's a lot to ask and I certainly don't want to intrude on any private or personal things you have to. I'll buy my own ticket, pay for my own hotel room. I'll stay out of your way as much as you want."

She stopped, took a deep breath then started again.

"Look Finn, to be completely honest, I can't bear the thought of being away from you for over a week. I know you probably want a break to catch a breath and get some perspective and I respect that. But selfishly, I just don't want to be away from you for that long. I even have a

passport that's never been used. If nothing else, it's high time I got some pages stamped."

She laughed.

"Okay, well, I admit that last part about the passport is a totally lame excuse but I'm willing to pull any rabbit out the hat that I can."

Finn looked at her. He couldn't help but laugh at her earnestness. At first, when she had spoken, he thought it was a terrible idea and that it had all the hallmarks of a potential disaster. Some many things could wrong and they'd be stuck with each other four thousand miles away from home.

However, as she had continued to speak, he began to change his mind and it seemed that maybe this might be the way to get their relationship over the line. If Bella had gone to Vegas to watch him fight knowing it was the very hardest thing for her to do, then he could take her Ireland which would be the very hardest place to be with her. Maybe, just maybe, he could finally put his ghosts to rest when they were there.

So, to Bella's amazement, she heard him say, "I think that's a great idea. Let's do it."

She was dumbfounded. She had practiced her arguments every day against the objections she was sure he would have. She had each point and counterpoint that she was going to make perfectly clear in her mind. Now, none of them were needed. He had agreed on the first go around.

Bella turned and leapt directly in to his arms with a force that nearly knocked him over then buried her face in his neck.

"Thank you, thank you, thank you!" she exclaimed joyously. "I was sure you'd say no."

"So was I but you're very persuasive. Besides, I guess I'd miss you too."

In the space of a few minutes, he had gone from wanting to put some space between them to realizing that he would actually miss her I he was alone in Ireland without her. He put her down and turned to face her.

"Should I ask Hank if it's okay with him?"

Bella rounded on him in amazement.

"What!" she spluttered. "I'm twenty-six years old. I'm pretty sure my grandfather won't have a problem."

"I'm sure you're right, Bella, but I don't want to upset him."

"Look Finn, I've already lived longer than the other important women in his life. I know he would want me to embrace every opportunity for happiness that comes my way."

Finn thought about that. While he knew about what she had said, it was only when she had put it like that that he had realized its significance. At twenty-six, Bella had already lived several years longer than her mother and her grandmother. It was an amazing concept to Finn.

"Okay, you win. I'll let you tell Hank."

Bella was still deliriously happy with herself.

"Okay. Now tell me exactly where you think we should go and what we should do when we're there. Christ, I can't believe it. I'm so happy. Thank you, thank you, thank you."

Finn was happy too. He had reservations but he was beginning to think this was the right call.

Chapter Thirty
July 1989
Ireland

Bella woke with a start. Her neck was stiff from the angle she had fallen asleep at. It took her a few moments to get her bearings then she looked out the window of the plane, just in time to see the coast of Ireland appearing in the distance. She turned to tell Finn but he was still fast asleep.

She looked at him with amusement. Each time he exhaled a little bubble would appear at one corner of his mouth, then recede only to reappear with his next breath. She had to admit that he did look very cute when he was sleeping. She was so excited and desperately wanted to wake him but she knew that wouldn't be fair so she let him be.

Besides, I'm pretty sure he's seen the coast of Ireland before, she thought with a smile.

Their journey had been relatively incident-free so far. Hank had driven them to the airport in Frankfort from where they were going to fly to New York then catch an Aer Lingus flight to Shannon. Bella had talked non-stop the whole way in the car. She could hardly contain her

excitement. Not only was she taking her first overseas trip but she was doing so with this wonderful man that she had fallen so deeply in love with. It was a virtual dream come true.

Hank and Finn had exchanged glances several times smiling at Bella's torrent of ideas and plans that she had charted out for their trip.

"You're trying to cram too much into each day," Finn had tried to warn her on several occasions. "There's no possible way of getting to see that many different places in such a short period of time. We'll also need to eat and sleep as well, you know."

But her enthusiasm was infectious and Finn had been swept up in it as the day approached closer and closer. On the plane now, Bella smiled when she thought about their disagreements over where they would visit and stay. Bella had wanted to map all this out in advance and make reservations before they left.

Finn, on the other hand, said they should play it by ear and not pin themselves down. He tried to persuade her that there were B&B's dotted all over Ireland and that putting a roof over their heads each night was not going to be a problem. Bella was dubious, and not being prepared in advance was completely against her nature, but eventually she bowed to Finn's superior local knowledge but not before warning him.

"Just so you know, the first night I have to sleep in a car will be the last night of peace you'll ever know. I just want to be sure we're perfectly clear on that point."

Finn had laughed.

"You'll see. It will be fine."

She felt him stir next to her and turned to smile at him.

"Good morning, sleepyhead. Welcome to Ireland."

Before he could respond, an announcement was made from the cockpit that they would be landing in ten minutes. Bella poked Finn with her finger.

"Did you hear that? Only ten minutes. Yippee!"

"Good morning yourself. I see your enthusiasm and excitement haven't waned one little bit. I don't know how you can keep the tempo up all the time."

Bella leaned closer to Finn and whispered conspiratorially in his ear, "It's love, lust, and hunger that spur me on. You think about that, dearest."

Finn feigned mock horror. Although, they still had not been intimate, they were certainly on that path towards it now and playful teasing with an underlying sexual innuendo was becoming a more frequent component of their interchanges.

"Promises, promises. Such a big mouth."

Just as he immediately realized what he had said, just then the big plane landed softly at Shannon Airport and Bella was distracted from making what Finn was sure would be another zinger. The captain made the announcement welcoming everyone to Ireland and, as was the custom on Aer Lingus, did it both in English and in Irish.

"What's he saying?" Bella asked Finn, unable to decipher even a single word of the announcement in Irish.

"Exactly the same thing he said in English," Finn responded. "Here's a bit of trivia for you now; did you know the Irish alphabet has only twenty-two letters and the word 'no' doesn't exist in the Irish language?"

But he had lost his audience, the plane door was being opened and Bella had pushed past him into the aisle and was in the process of retrieving her stuff from the overhead compartment. Finn shrugged. "Never mind. It will keep."

"Did you say something, Finn?"

"Yes, welcome to Ireland, Bella Cartwright Holder. Please allow me the great honor of being the first person to kiss you on Irish soil."

He reached over and kissed Bella softly on the lips.

"Mmm," she murmured. "I think your lips might actually taste nicer over here. I could get to like this."

Their luggage arrived quickly and fifteen minutes later they were sitting in the rental car. Bella was fascinated by the steering wheel being on the other side of what she was used to and the stick shift gears looked like too much of a challenge for her to even contemplate driving.

"I'm glad you're the one driving," she declared. "I'm not sure I'd be up for this. Hey, are you sure you're not too tired? You haven't slept much and we've been traveling a long time. God, I'd kill for a shower or a nice long bath. I feel so grotty. What's the plan, man?"

She had jumbled all those themes into one seemingly long sentence while Finn was studying a map he had opened out. He looked at her now distractedly.

"Huh? What was that?"

"Nothing of importance. I was just checking if you were sufficiently awake and alert to drive so that we don't end up in a ditch or go right off a cliff. Not that big of a deal."

"I'm fine, Bella. Let's drive south towards Kerry for a few hours, then find a B&B and rest up. Deal?"

"You got it, man. Let's go already."

Chapter Thirty-One
July 1989
Ireland

Bella would later declare that the next five days were the absolute best of her life so far. They had first headed south to Kerry as planned. Their initial stop was Dingle where Bella had her very first experience of Guinness and a breakfast that was known locally as a 'full Irish'. They had decided to recharge their batteries with some food and drink at Ashe's Pub, which was one of the most popular of the very many pubs Dingle had to offer.

Bella was amazed at the sheer number of pubs all concentrated in one location and serving what to her was the population of little more than a village.

"But why so many?" she had asked. "Do they all do business?"

"It's a long story," Finn replied. "But yes, they all do business. We can try them all if you want proof."

She had really liked the taste of Guinness from her first sip.

"Maybe there's a bit of Irish in me, after all," she declared after she smacked her lips with enjoyment at the

smooth creamy taste of a perfectly poured pint that had come resplendent with a shamrock outlined in its head. Then she looked mischievously at Finn and whispered suggestively in his ear, "And I'd really like a bit more Irish in me sometime soon."

Finn shook with laughter at that. She really had a quick wit and a dirty mind. He enjoyed both. For all her enthusiasm about Guinness though, she was more than a little uncertain about the 'full Irish'. She peered at the plate skeptically, sniffed at it then finally tentatively poked at its contents with a nervous expression on her face.

The sausage she got and so too the bacon but the black and white puddings, the fried mushroom, and the runniest egg she had ever seen, fazed her. Not to mention the big scoop of baked beans that covered a section of the plate.

"I don't know about this at all. Maybe I'll stick to the Guinness. It looks and tastes like a meal unto itself."

"Trust me, Bella," Finn had said encouragingly. "I promise you this, you'll love it. Try it with the toast and it'll amaze you."

She started nibbling tentatively but soon, as Finn had predicted, she was gulping it down.

"My God, this is so delicious."

She happily blurted out as a trail of egg made its way down her chin. She wiped at it with some toast rather than waste it.

And so it continued over the next few days as they made their way lazily around the Ring of Kerry and on into West Cork. There were other highlights along the way. They had climbed to the top of Mount Brandon, the second highest mountain in Ireland, from which the views were

spectacular. Then they raced each other down the steep track, laughing and tumbling most of the way.

Another big moment, and one that left Bella feeling more than a little disappointed, occurred when they visited Garnish Island, a small picturesque island located in Glengarriff Harbor, which is itself part of Bantry Bay. The island is accessible only by ferry boat from the village of Glengarriff and Finn suggested they go there to see the beautiful collection of flowers and plants, many of which do not grow anywhere else in the country.

They had spent the day wandering happily through the gardens and forests and completely lost track of time. When they finally arrived at the dock, they discovered to their shock that it was completely deserted and there was no boat anywhere to be seen. Finn looked at his watch and realized that they had missed the last ferry by over thirty minutes. He looked over at Bella.

"Damn it. We're screwed. We're going to be stuck here for the night, no food, no shelter."

He sat on a rock dejectedly staring over at the distant village. This was not going to be fun.

"Well now, I'm not worried," she teased. "Because my big hero is going to build a fire, hunt down some wild animal or maybe even a rabbit, and roast it up. Afterwards, he's going to build a big shelter with his bare hands using vines and fallen trees to keep us perfectly warm tonight. That is what's going to happen, right?"

"Not funny, Bella. You won't be quite as happy when the sun goes down and it will be completely dark out here."

Bella didn't respond but thought to herself, *That's where you're wrong, Finn. I actually will be very happy to be stranded here alone all night with you.*

She was lost in that happy thought when Finn jumped up and shouted, "Yes, look Bella. There's someone coming."

Bella smiled back at him but she was not at all happy with the conscientious ferryboat skipper who had realized that the beautiful black woman he had transported out to the island that morning had not come back in the afternoon. If Bella had been anyone else, they would have been stuck on the island for the night.

Finn had put that experience in the lucky break column but there had been others that he had truly enjoyed. They had gone for a walk on a beach one afternoon that was near the B&B they were staying in that night. Bella confessed that it her very first experience of being at a beach as she had never even seen the sea before.

With that, Finn had scooped her up in his arms and charged headlong into the sea until they were waist high and unceremoniously dumped her into the water. She had stood up coughing and spluttering from the shock of the cold water in her face and its saltiness in her mouth and her eyes.

"You fucking asshole!" she shouted. "I could have drowned. I can't swim, you know. Prick."

But Finn had just laughed and dunked her again.

"You won't drown, Bella. I got you."

She was so mad that she began to laugh herself and splashed water at him. They had stayed there for ten minutes until their soaking wet clothes began to stick uncomfortably to them. He had also gotten a kick out of the time when they

were driving along some back roads and Bella desperately needed to pee.

"Aren't there any pubs or gas stations nearby?" she had groaned, crossing her legs tightly.

"Not for about twenty or miles or so."

"I can't last twenty miles. What am I going to do? I won't make it."

Finn pulled over to the side of the road and nodded at a field. "Climb in there, go behind a bush. No one will see you."

"You want me to pee in someone's field?"

"I don't think they'll mind or even know for that matter."

She groaned again. Then opened the car door.

"You stay here. No peeking. I don't need an audience."

"Okay. I'll stay right here."

About thirty seconds later, he heard her screaming his name desperately. He got out of the car to see what was wrong. There was absolutely nobody around so it couldn't be that. She screamed again.

"Finn, help. These beasts are coming for me. They're so frigging scary."

"I thought you said I had to stay here."

"Forget that. Quickly, they're looking at me evilly."

Finn truly wished he had a camera when he saw Bella crouching terrified behind a bush in mortal fear of about six cows who were looking at her curiously.

"They're cows, Bella. They won't touch you. They're just curious that's all. It's not often they see an American woman peeing on their lawn."

"Make them go away," she wailed. "I'm not moving until you do."

Finn sighed, hopped over the gate, and quickly dispersed the cows.

"We good?"

"Yes, thank you. I tell you those beasts are evil."

Now, finally they were heading up towards the graveyard where Finn's wife and daughter were buried. This was the part of the trip that Bella had been dreading more than anything else for she knew how heart wrenching it would be for Finn. She had told him that she wouldn't mind if he didn't bring her there with him but he had been adamant that it was important for all of them to be there together.

As they drove along, she grew silent and the knot in her stomach got harder and harder. They had planned to stop in Ballinasloe for the night and then make the journey out west to the cemetery early the next morning. It was very late when they got there and they drove to Hayden's hotel, which was the only one the town had to offer.

When they went to reception desk, they were informed that there was only a single room. The receptionist seemed surprised when this news was not well received by the guests. Finn turned to at Bella.

"Do you want to keep going? We can try the next town."

She shook her head. "Finn, it's late, I'm bushed. Besides, it has two beds. It will be fine."

Finn looked at her intently. They had agreed that there would be no room sharing on this trip to avoid complications and he really didn't need to break that agreement the night before he visited his family's grave.

197

Still it was very late and the room did have two beds. He would just have to trust her. He turned to the receptionist.

"We'll take it, thanks."

The receptionist's expression was inscrutable as he handed over the key but Finn could almost see the man wishing he was the one spending the night with Bella.

The room was clean but compact with two double beds. They were in bed in less than ten minutes. Finn was asleep in another five. For Bella this was the closest she had ever come to sleeping with a man so she just lay there listening to Finn breathing, aching for him.

The next morning, Finn was awoken by the bright sunlight streaming through a crack in the curtains. He almost jumped with shock when he saw and felt Bella snuggled up against him wearing only her underwear. He racked his brains trying to recollect how this had come about but all he could remember was getting into bed by himself and falling asleep quickly.

He looked at her lying there, all peaceful and content. She looked so adorable with her mussed up hair spread over the pillow that he decided to just lie there and not wake her. Almost subconsciously, his eyes began to travel over her body. He followed the curve of her neck down to her shoulders to her breasts. He watched them rise and swell as she breathed gently. He could see the outline of her dark nipples through her bra.

Then his eyes moved down her taut, flat belly and he could see the lightest dusting of very fine hair form a trail from her navel to her crotch. He looked at the outline of her mound as it protruded from her panties then finally, he traveled down her long and beautiful legs. He repeated the

journey back up her body only to find Bella lying there wide awake, looking directly into his eyes.

"Did you enjoy the tour?" she asked innocently. "I sure hope you got your money's worth because you seemed to be traveling slowly."

"Oh God, I'm sorry, Bella. I didn't mean…I mean—"

She put her finger to his lips and said, "Shush. Don't speak. I know this may not exactly be the morning to say this but you can take that tour anytime you want with your eyes, your mouth, your hands or anything else you want to use. And I think you know that."

"Besides," she continued, "you're probably wondering how I got to be lying in your bed in only my underwear."

"I was curious about that because I have no recollection whatsoever."

Bella snuggled in closer to him and replied, "Okay, I can give you the story I've concocted or I can tell you the truth. Which do you want?"

"How about we start with the story and follow up with the truth?"

"Okay. Well, as the story goes, you were having a really bad dream. So much so that you became inconsolable. I tried everything I could to wake to no avail. The only that seemed to calm you was when I snuggled up to you, which I did. After a while, I fell asleep.

"Then I woke up and I was really hot so I decided to go back to my own bed but as I left you got upset again so I simply removed my pajamas and snuggled back in next to you. I had planned to leave before the morning came but I guess I overslept. What do you think? Plausible?"

"I'd say you'd get away with that in a court of law. And the truth?"

"Ah, yes. The truth. The truth is much more sordid. I lay there listening to you sleeping and I wanted you so much that I took off my pajamas and climbed in next to you. I was sure you'd wake up and hunt me out but you kept sleeping. I thought this might well be my only chance to share a bed with you and I had to take it. I did, however, plan to be gone by morning, but as I said, I overslept."

Finn ruffled her hair.

"I'll take that one actually. I like it better. Now, however, we should get going. Do you want to shower first?"

She hugged him tightly for a moment then got out of bed.

"I won't be long."

When she was in the shower, Finn just lay there thinking. He was feeling very guilty and he was back to being unsure about his whole relationship with Bella. He had really enjoyed the week with her but now it was almost like he had crossed over a line and didn't really like what he saw on the other side. It was all so confusing.

After a light breakfast, they headed west. The weather was absolutely glorious and they drove along with all the windows open enjoying the warm air that flowed into the car. They were both lost in their thoughts so they rode along in complete silence.

Bella was worried that this was it. She was concerned that they would go the cemetery and Finn would realize that he couldn't get past the memories of his dead family and

would just let her go. She told herself that she would accept the outcome either way.

They stopped at a little store to buy flowers and potted plants and then they were there in the parking lot outside the cemetery.

"Do you want me to wait here?" Bella asked quietly.

"No, I want you to come with me, please."

They walked along the gravel path to the far corner where the grave was located. The sound of their shoes crunching the stones seemed so loud and out of place to Bella. She had to admit that the location was spectacular; gently sloping mountains forming a protective barrier on one side and the ocean on the other sending the faintest smell of salt into the air with each crashing wave.

Finn had told her how he had searched carefully for this location. Julia had wanted to be buried in a place like this but he hadn't expected to have find one so soon.

When they got to the grave, they first cleaned away some dead flowers and pulled up a few weeds growing along the edges. Then they placed the fresh flowers in a vase and put the potted plants just in front of the headstone. After that, they sat back on the little concrete ledge that went around the grave. There was no one else around and the place was in complete silence. Finn spoke first.

"Hi Julia, hi baby Siodhraidh. It's been a long while I know and I'm sorry for that. I want you both to know though I absolutely haven't forgotten you guys, at all. I think of you both every day, how much I miss you and how much I love you. And I know it's so nice being here with you but, honestly, seeing you both lying here, separated like this from me; well that's so hard to deal with and it hurts an

awful lot. I guess, I'm just not brave enough to come more often because of that but I promise I'll try to."

His voice had choked up and he struggled to continue. Bella sat next to him, weeping silently.

"Anyway, I brought a friend this time. Her name is Bella. I think you'd both like her. I like her and I've been spending a lot of time with her lately. I wanted you guys to meet her and for her to meet you. You see I'm stuck in this very complicated situation. I feel like my heart is buried here with you guys and locked away forever but I also want to be fair to Bella. I can't be with her if there's nowhere in my heart for her to be. So there it is. I'm kind of stuck and I was hoping to find some answers here today."

Finn paused. His heart was thumping wildly. This had been a terrible mistake. What did he think was going to happen? Had he expected some sign from the grave or from the heavens giving or refusing permission? It was stupid. As he sat there berating himself, he heard Bella begin to speak in a soft and dignified voice.

"Hello Julia and Siodhraidh. This is Bella. I'm so happy Finn brought me here to this beautiful place to meet you. I'm going to be honest with you. I'm totally in love with this wonderful man and I'd like nothing better than to spend the rest of my life with him. But I also want you to know that I don't want to replace either of you in his life nor would I ever try to take him away from you both.

"He's yours first and foremost and that will never change for me. I would be so happy if you could find a way for him to understand that my love comes with complete acceptance of his family and all I'm asking is to become a

part of that. I don't want to be with him instead of you. I want to be with him alongside you and as part of you."

Bella could feel how emotional Finn was getting but she continued.

"You know, I really don't know how Finn feels about me and that's okay. I'm willing to wait for as long as it takes. I just hope that someday, in time, he might grow to love me even just a little bit as much as I love him. That's all I'm hoping for because with that we could have a really happy life together and I promise I'll take real good care of him."

Bella stopped talking. The pain she felt here the grave side was so overwhelming. It was almost like she could reach out and touch it with her hand, it so tangible. Her voice quivered as she spoke again.

"I'm going to go now and give you guys some time to be alone together. I'm so pleased I got to meet you and I really hope I get to come here again. Bye for now."

Bella stood up and dusted herself down with her hands. As she did, it seemed to her as if she was brushing away all the fractured uncertainties in her life. It was almost as if thousands of moving parts seamlessly interlocked to form a whole new structure, she could almost physically sense them clicking into place.

In a most curious turn of events, here in a cemetery in the West of Ireland, Bella Cartwright Holder became free of the tangled grasp her family's history had kept on her until now. With that simple act of brushing dust from her clothes, it seemed like she cleaned away decades of shame and sadness that surrounded her family and had seemingly been passed from one generation to another without fail.

She had broken that cycle now through the honesty and strength of her love for a man that she could lose any minute now.

"I…"

But she stopped. There was nothing really to say now. Words would be completely redundant. Finn had kept his head down the whole time, neither looking at her nor at the grave. She nodded and walked away. He would come to her or he would not. She would find out soon and, either way, she would be fine.

Finn turned to look at her as she walked down the gravel path. He watched the fluid dignity in her stride and could see the strength in the straightness of her back. He knew what an effort it had been for her to say what she did. Not many people would have the courage to want join a family like his under these circumstances.

He just didn't know what to do. He looked at the headstone and said, "Jules?"

Then sat there as if he was waiting for a response. After about ten minutes, he decided it was time to go and tell Bella that he could not be with her. It wasn't that he didn't want to be with her, it was that he couldn't. He started to walk towards her. He had gone about ten paces when he heard, or thought he heard, a slight noise. He turned back to look and saw that a flower had tumbled out of the vase onto the grave. It was a rose.

At that moment, a vision of Julia standing on the altar on their wedding day, singing the song *The Rose* came clearly into his mind. It had been one of her favorites. She had loved the idea that despite all of the trials and tribulations of life, love would always shine through and

new seeds of hope would be revealed by the melting snow. He walked back to the grave and replaced the flower. He now knew had he had been given his answer. He stood and looked at the headstone for a few minutes then gently ran his fingers across their names.

All he simply said was, "Thank you."

He started to walk. Bella could hear him coming towards him but she kept staring straight ahead. With each step bringing him closer, it seemed like her heart was getting ready to explode. When Finn reached the bench where she was sitting, he stopped and put out his hand. Bella looked up at him, desperately trying to see what it meant but there were no clues to be found on his face.

She stood up and took his outstretched hand and they headed towards the entrance. Out of habit, she rubbed his thumb with hers then asked, "Are you okay?"

They walked on for a little bit before she heard his reply.

"I will be. In time."

Epilogue

Eight months later, Bella and Finn were married in the grounds of the Cartwright estate in Strongville, Georgia, where they now live.